# Gemini Trip

**Books by Janice Law**

The Big Payoff
Gemini Trip

# Gemini Trip

## Janice Law

Houghton Mifflin Company
Boston 1977

Copyright © 1977 by Janice Law

All rights reserved. No part of this work may be
reproduced or transmitted in any form by any
means, electronic or mechanical, including
photocopying and recording, or by any
information storage or retrieval system, without
permission in writing from the publisher.

Library of Congress Cataloging in Publication Data

Law, Janice.
    Gemini trip.
    I. Title.
PZ4.L415Ge    [PS3562.A86]    813'.5'4    77–7614
ISBN 0–395–25703–4

*Printed in the United States of America*
s 10 9 8 7 6 5 4 3 2 1

**For Jerry**

# Gemini Trip

# Chapter 1

Any day that includes a summons from your boss is bad, but this one had looked dubious from the beginning. Before ten A.M., I had learned that my invaluable secretary needed six more months with her baby, that the air conditioner was dying, and that the copying department had shredded an important report. At ten, the day took on a truly funereal complexion: Bertrand Gilson wanted to see me.

"Did he say why?"

"No, Miss Peters. He just said it was 'urgent and confidential.'"

Worse and worse. Gilson is the chairman of the board. An audience with him is almost invariably unpleasant, but I had other reasons for avoiding him. Nothing personal — in fact, I rather admired him — just strategic. Gilson had given me my highly lucrative job. I deserved it, but the circumstances had been . . . unusual. Sooner or later he was going to want something in return, and for over a year I'd been waiting to see what that might be.

When I arrived at his secretary's desk, I got the first of several surprises. No "take a seat," no "just a few minutes please."

"Mr. Gilson will see you right away," Amelia Braun snapped. Miss Braun is a tiny martinet with black eyes and white hair who compresses the disposition of Attila the Hun into five feet of bones, powder, and corset. From her post at Gilson's door, she amuses herself by intimidating everyone in the company, from the oldest member of the board to the youngest custodian. As I followed her quick steps into the office, I wondered if she were responsible for my summons.

Inside, a glass wall stretched from the plush carpet to the acoustical tiles, affording a panoramic view of Washington and

# 2

throwing a bright glare on visitors. The great man was lounging in his swivel chair, staring reflectively out at the late summer haze and ignoring the folders and the piles of loose papers on his desk.

"Miss Peters, sir," Miss Braun announced. Then she shut the door, and Gilson stood up and shook my hand.

"Good to see you again, Miss Peters. We've been getting excellent reports about your work. How are you liking it?"

"Very much, sir. If I may say so, it's the ideal position for me."

Gilson smiled slyly. He is a rotund gentleman who expands from small, almost fragile, extremities to an impressive midsection and a bold red face. Despite his jovial appearance, he is a consummate master of company politics, a shrewd psychologist, and an actor with a real flair for executive theatrics. I enjoyed his performances when I wasn't personally involved, and even today I was curious to see who would take the stage. It was the friendly, fatherly Grand Old Man of the Company. Beware of that one. We discussed various bits of company news, and I waited to see what the GOM had up his sleeve. It turned out to be the Queen of Spades.

"Do you remember Morgan Blythe?" he asked after a while.

"He was before my time, I think. What department was he in?"

"He was on the board. His father headed the South Texas Corporation, and when we merged, Morgan came on here. He was a brilliant engineer. Some of our offshore equipment was designed by his firm."

"That would be the BLX line, wouldn't it?"

"Correct. Morgan did the initial work on that. His death was a great loss. A very great loss indeed."

"Was this recent?"

"No, no. Ten years ago, at least. He was killed in a private plane crash in Delaware."

Gilson lapsed into silence. I had some questions but decided not to ask them. The haze outside took on a whitish cast as the sun rose higher. I hoped my air conditioner would soon be fixed.

"Morgan left two children," Gilson resumed, "twins, Crystal and Edward. They turn twenty-one this year on" — he consulted a stack of papers on his desk — "the thirtieth of September. That's the problem."

"The problem, sir?"

"Miss Peters," Gilson began in his best chairman-of-the-board voice, "we have here a peculiar and highly confidential matter." He paused to give me the sort of smile that usually accompanies one's imminent annihilation. "The kind of thing to which you're no stranger."

My wait was over. Gilson was about to make me pay for my job. "I've had varied business experiences."

"This is in the 'varied' category. Morgan Blythe's mother inherited most of the family fortune. Morgan was making enough on his own, and in any case, his early death eliminated him as an heir. His wife, Sybil, will not inherit the Blythe money. She was never a stable person, and since Morgan's death — " He gestured. "You will see, anyway. The Blythe fortune is extremely large and significantly entangled with New World Oil, Miss Peters. It must be well managed."

"Are the twins the heirs?"

"Yes. And here's where you come in, Miss Peters. Old Mrs. Blythe is in a nursing home at the moment. She is not expected to live much longer. Within a month or so, Crystal and Edward Blythe will become two of the richest young people in the country."

"A nice way to begin adult life."

"Perhaps, but they must be here, and if possible, they should be under the guidance of sound financial advisers."

"Preferably ours?"

"Ah, you're a shade too Machiavellian. That's premature. First they must be here."

"And where are they?"

"Edward is in Paris. He and his sister have lived there, doing

God knows what, for the last two years. Sybil has no more control over them than she has over anything else. Their lives have been, shall we say, irregular."

He pronounced the word as if it were a contagious disease. "And where is Crystal?"

"That, Miss Peters, is what you are going to find out."

"Me? I can't leave the office to go to Paris. Surely there are detectives to find missing persons, even missing heiresses."

He cut me off sharply. "Miss Peters, I have mentioned the unfortunate instability of Mrs. Blythe. According to my last conversation with her, the girl may not even be missing. She may be vacationing in Normandy. It is very difficult with Sybil Blythe," he said irascibly, "to tell what is going on. My own opinion, which she did not care to hear, was that the children were playing irresponsible games. It would not be the first time. Were they mine, I would handle the situation differently, but they're not, and Sybil could make a great deal of trouble if she's crossed. So I'm sure you can see the delicacy of the task and the very great advantages of having someone from New World involved."

"Yes, that's obvious, but we have a department full of people who are trained in" — I hesitated. It's not always easy to discuss the Special Accounts people with the top brass — "finding out things and turning up people."

"This is a delicate matter," Gilson said, pausing to give me another sly smile. "It requires a woman's touch."

"We have no women in Special Accounts?"

"Try to curb your feminist instincts for the moment, Miss Peters," he replied crossly. "At the risk of turning your head, I can say that you're the person we need. I know your objections. You don't need to worry. This isn't an attempt to remove you from the Research Department. You can take my word for that. And even if you are an amateur at this sort of affair, you have an uncanny knack for finding out what others want to keep hidden."

Understanding his reference, I made an attempt to be conciliatory. "Yes. Well, if Miss Blythe were in this country

— or even in Britain — I would be very happy to help, but France! In a matter as 'delicate' as this one, surely you need someone who speaks the language fluently."

Gilson cleared his throat. "You had, let me see, two years of French in high school, and you took a course we offered your first year with the company. Am I right?"

"I can order dinner and follow French movies. That's not enough to solicit information, especially from people who have no reason to confide in me. I strongly recommend you find a French-speaking detective."

Gilson waved his hand imperiously. "Any fool can speak French — many do. A good part of this continent, in fact. I will provide you with an interpreter. If you understand enough to know if he is doing his job correctly, that will be sufficient."

My heart sank. He was serious.

"I will mention only one other thing," Gilson continued. "The Blythes are old friends of Henry Brammin's. He contacted me about the matter in the first place."

Henry Brammin was my friend, benefactor, and first employer at New World. I owed him a lot.

"I see," I replied. The trip to Paris looked like a certainty.

Gilson noted my change of expression. "I thought that would make a difference," he remarked. "Well, when could you leave?"

"I could leave tomorrow, but it might be better to take a few days to talk to the family and to some of the Blythe girl's friends."

"I quite agree." He produced some papers. "Read these over. They are letters from Henry and Mrs. Blythe and a list of Crystal's friends."

"What about her governess, or nanny, or whatever? A young heiress isn't entrusted to nonprofessionals, is she?"

Gilson frowned. "I will have Miss Braun inquire. Could you leave within the week?"

I looked over the list of names. Crystal Blythe had not been burdened with many friends. "Yes, although there will be some traveling involved."

"Good, and there's another thing." He brushed an imaginary crumb from his immaculate suit. "Who would you like to take with you?"

"With me?"

"Certainly," he replied smoothly. "Of course, this isn't really company business. You're going on a two-week vacation. Stay at a nice hotel, eat well, make a few discreet inquiries as a friend of a friend of the family. Do nothing to suggest that you've come especially to round up the two young fools and bring them home." He made a sour face. I got the impression that he had dealt with the Blythes in the past. "Do you understand what's required?"

I wasn't sure. "You do expect me to find her, though?"

"That goes without saying. I don't expect it will be too hard. That young man of yours — he's an artist, isn't he?" he asked casually.

I nodded. I didn't like this at all.

"Well then, what's the problem? A splendid city for the arts. Now, I was thinking of putting in Jim Eddison while you're gone."

He was a cheerful nonentity. "A good choice," I said.

Gilson had it all set up. "Ah, from your point of view, yes. Don't be gone too long, though. Now, there are a few other things you should know . . ."

*

"Try to get those reservations made today."

She counted off on her fingers: "That's one to Hartford and a car, confirm a hotel in Charlottesville, and two tickets for a flight to Paris within six days. Anything else?"

"No. I'll take my own car on the trip to Virginia. You'll have to call first and check with Mrs. Blythe about my coming. Braun has already been in contact with her, so mention her name and Gilson's."

"This Jim Eddison, is he nice?"

I sighed. When would my own secretary get back? "He's very nice, rather slow, and has a wife and three kids."

Her face fell. I couldn't blame her. It's discouraging how few men are both attractive and single, but that was her problem; mine was Crystal Blythe. I read through the letters, then tried to figure out how I would find a rich, spoiled, eccentric young woman in a country where I could barely communicate, where I knew no one, and where I had to pass as a tourist, *avec le boyfriend,* no less. That raised another problem: Harry. Mixing business and family (which Harry is, as far as I've got one at all) is no good. I didn't like it. Still, Gilson was right. It was the right approach if the Blythes were to be handled delicately. I leaned back in my chair and stared at a ceramic in the shape of a half-squashed pack of Camels. How I wanted a cigarette! That china glob was a replica of the last pack I'd bought. Harry had made it as a joke. Damn him and the surgeon general, too. I decided that a man who convinces you to give up smoking deserves all he gets. Poor Harry or lucky Harry — Gilson was right. He'd find a trip to Paris irresistible.

\*

The window air conditioner cut in with a wheezing, sucking noise. I opened my eyes. Outside the high window, the city sky was a murky semisolid tinged with lavender. I settled my head comfortably into the smooth, warm hollow between Harry's chest and shoulder. He stretched a little and said, "That apartment was too small. No room for a press."

We'd been looking for an apartment large enough for both of us. "That's too bad. But I told you, my tenant's lease is up in the spring."

"No garage there."

"No rent, either." I own a duplex near Georgetown.

"I'd have to look into renting a garage in that case."

"Yes, you would."

A shadow fluttered across the ceiling as the breeze from the air conditioner lifted the curtains.

"I saw your fairy godmother today."

"Oh, yeah? How is she?" Harry asked.

"He's alive and well and working at New World Oil."

"One of those, huh? I didn't know the petrocombine went in for transvestites."

"Your fairy godmother, surprisingly enough, has turned out to be Bertrand Gilson. Do you remember him? He came to see you after that mess in Scotland."

"Sure. What about him?"

"He wants to give you a trip to Paris."

"You're kidding!"

"Not entirely. Could you get some time off? All expenses paid, and we'd leave in a week."

"All expenses paid to Paris? I certainly could! But there's got to be a catch somewhere."

"There is, but not for you. You can do anything you want, short of running away with an exotic dancer."

"I wouldn't think I'd have time for that. I'd want to see all the museums again, of course, and there are dozens of commercial galleries. How long would we stay?"

"Two weeks at the most."

"Two weeks — that will take some planning." He sat up with a jerk, sending my head thumping down onto the mattress.

"Ouch."

"Sorry." He turned on the light and began rummaging through a bookcase.

"You don't care to hear about the catch in the plan?"

"Hmmm. Nothing during gallery hours, I hope?"

"Well, I don't think so."

He leaned over and rubbed my head affectionately. "Nothing nasty this time? I mean nothing like the British business?"

"No, nothing like that. Work, though." I explained about Crystal Blythe.

Harry stretched out on the bed, his head propped on his hand. "You'll probably find the kid, won't you?"

"If she's tired of playing games. The family's dotty, from what I can tell."

"Doesn't Gilson know that?"

"Sure. It's just politicking. You know the sort of thing: 'We can assure you, Mrs. Blythe, we've done everything in our power, dispatched the head of our Research Department, blah, blah, blah.' Besides, he feels I owe him one after Scotland."

"You couldn't refuse?"

"Not very easily. And the Blythes are friends of old Brammin's."

"So I get a trip to Paris?"

"So you get a trip to Paris. I'll be honest, Harry, I don't like the setup, but it makes sense given what they want done, and since you love Paris, you may as well accept the ticket. If they're going to put me on the spot, at least we can have some fun at company expense."

"That's been one of my great ambitions: enjoying you at someone else's expense."

"That shows you're a frivolous Bohemian at heart."

"Nonsense," Harry said, pulling me closer, "United Graphics can survive without me. I'm going to live off my patron, New World Oil, for a while. The Jeu de Paume, the Louvre, the Orangerie — you'll love that — the Rodin Museum, the Art Moderne . . . I can't wait for you to see the Degas collection and the Monets. God bless missing heiresses. We'll have a wonderful time."

# Chapter 2

THE BLYTHES ARE ONE OF THOSE families that are followed in the newspapers with *of*'s — of such and such an island, of such and such a harbor, spring, dale, and Fifth Avenue address. Scattered that year by time and circumstance, the family had left only one Blythe at its summer residence, and as I drove through western Connecticut, poor Sybil seemed lost, too. The superhighway had long since given way to a two-lane blacktop populated largely by one-speed hay wagons, farm boys with souped-up trucks, and bike hikers from Camp Whatuwillee and similar linguistic monstrosities. This artery at last contracted to a single lane and then to a country dirt road with a high stony crown and treacherous shoulders. On either side the hedgerows grew in lush tangles, and beyond, in boulder-strewn pastures, Holsteins and Swiss Dairy ambled in the August heat. I pulled over, consulted my directions, and decided to persist for another mile. There was a dense woodlot at the end of one meadow, and near it the car purred gratefully onto a stretch of asphalt. Through the trees I saw a waterfall tumbling, slow and erratic in the late summer drought, out of a dark pond shaded by oak and hemlock. A drive led from the water, and at the roadside was an ornamental iron gatepost of fanciful design.

I turned in, and the rented car sputtered as it negotiated the steep drive in low, spinning its wheels and scattering the gravel. On the far bank of the pond was a handsome whitewashed-brick house of vaguely Georgian inspiration. French windows ran along its lower story, neatly pruned ornamentals flanked the door, and two huge stone basins in front were bursting with pink and blue annuals. An ugly bull mastiff slept in their shade. When I got out of the car, the dog raised its white-flecked muzzle and rose stiffly on arthritic legs, showing its remaining teeth in a canine grin, and watched me rap on the door. A dry, nimble, little woman in mouse-colored silk and a white apron emerged.

"I'm Anna Peters from New World Oil. Mrs. Blythe is expecting me."

"Come in. I'll tell Madam," she said.

I stepped into a hallway lined with fine old paneling, antique tables, and oriental pots. The maid returned almost at once to lead me to a large and beautiful room overlooking a rose garden. The warm air smelled of flowers, and the uninhibited summer chintz repeated the reds and pinks and greens of the garden, while underfoot a faded Aubusson lay as smooth and soft as moss. A woman dressed in a loose white kimono was lounging on one of the couches, drinking some clear colorless liquid.

"Welcome, Miss Peters. Martha, bring Miss Peters some lemonade." Her voice was at once languorous and brittle, like the loops and curls of fine-spun taffy.

I said "Good afternoon" and sat down. Bees were humming around the flowers, and in a nearby field a combine started. My hostess sipped her drink, and we considered each other. At forty-five or fifty, Sybil Blythe was a pretty woman who was not so much aging as being slowly erased — by time, trouble, or dissipation, I could not judge. Her fair skin was transparent even in the middle of summer, and her pale blonde hair and white silk costume faded into the room's pale walls and the faint off-white background of the chintz. The only spots of color in her face were a pair of dark blue eyes that must once have been extraordinary but now were distant and somehow unsettling. Unsettling because her fair, bland looks belonged with serenity, but despite the pastoral setting, serenity had long since departed.

"Berty's a very amusing man, don't you think?"

"Berty? Bertrand Gilson?"

"Yes, of course. Don't you know him well?"

I shook my head.

"Charming, though, sending you all this way. He really shouldn't have."

"Mr. Gilson told me you were concerned about your daughter."

"Oh, I probably talked too much. I am a *tiny* bit worried, but it's nothing serious. We were at a party, and with all the young people there, I just thought Crystal should be there, too! She was always the heart of any party."

"If you haven't heard from your daughter for a while, it's natural for you to be worried."

"I'm not worried," she insisted. "I'm not worried."

"But you do want Crystal located?"

"Berty says you can be discreet. Is that true?"

"Discretion is my business, Mrs. Blythe."

"This is not the ordinary sort of inquiry," she said quickly. "My daughter is an exceptional girl in every way. Both my children are. They have to be handled intelligently."

"Bertrand Gilson and Henry Brammin asked me to come and see you as a personal favor. I might as well tell you that this is not my usual line of work. If you don't feel confident about putting the matter in my hands, you are perfectly free to find someone else."

Annoyance wasn't becoming to Mrs. Blythe. It showed up the faded skin just under her eyes and the weakening of her jawline. "I understand. I'm just not used to this, you see."

"That is precisely why Mr. Gilson asked me to see you. Since you dislike the idea of a professional investigator, tell me about Crystal, and I will try to find her. The first thing would be to show me some pictures of her. Mr. Gilson didn't have any."

"That's Berty. Never has the essentials. Here — " She patted the cushion beside her. "Bring over the album next to you."

There were two leatherbound books on the coffee table. I picked them up.

"The older one is of no interest to you," she said sharply.

"All right." I put down the more faded of the two volumes and brought the other. She opened it and pointed to two fat babies sitting in a carriage pushed by a sturdy, red-faced woman.

"There are my darlings. And Duncan with them, of course. She stayed until they were five. Then Mademoiselle Chantell came." She turned the soft black pages. The babies left their carriage and transformed fat into fair, sun-dappled arms and long, tanned legs with bony knees. They sat on ponies and sleds and posed in summer whites before opulent gardens. They flanked their mastiff on a spotless beach and played with an assortment of expensive toys. As they grew, Mrs. Blythe talked without saying anything, and in her languid voice something whispered nervously, aren't they perfect? aren't they exquisite? how could things ever go wrong? The last pages confirmed the young Blythes' childish promise. Edward, tall and broad-shouldered, lounged in a hammock, while Crystal, long fair hair falling over her shoulders, adjusted the sails of a small boat. Their beauty was indeed surprising.

"Do they enjoy sailing?"

"Oh, yes, Crystal's very fond of the water."

"What about Edward?"

"Edward never cared for boats. Those were taken in Maine, two years ago. The summer before they left for Europe."

"And they've been in Paris ever since?"

"I've seen them on vacations." Mrs. Blythe sipped more of the clear liquid. "They're at the Sorbonne, studying," she added. She didn't sound completely confident.

"Do they both speak French well?"

"Perfectly. Like Parisians."

"When were they home last?"

"Last Christmas we were all in New York. I went to see them. It was very cold and disagreeable in the city. So dirty."

"Yes, I'm sure. Were they both well? In good spirits, I mean."

"Of course. I told you, my daughter is a joyous person."

"And Edward?"

"Yes, yes, Edward too, but you know, in a boy . . ."

"Yes?"

"Well, a little more sobriety is in order. A more solid impression. And Edward is so good at giving the correct impression, always. In his own way he is remarkable," she hurried on. "You will understand when you meet him."

"I see." During the ensuing silence I considered Mrs. Blythe's peculiar description of her son. She had curiously little to say about her children's current situation. "You mentioned that they were at the Sorbonne. What were they studying?"

"They *are* at the Sorbonne," she corrected. "Oh, the usual, I suppose. They are both enchanted with the arts." She pronounced the phrase as if it were the name of an expensive perfume.

"In particular?"

"Writing. They're both very literary, very verbal. And Crystal used to paint, too. Such interesting things." Every other word was italicized. It made me wonder.

"Are they good students?"

"I told you, my children are quite exceptional," Mrs. Blythe protested in irritation. "You people are all the same — no imagination, no appreciation for the inner life." More italics. She had a whole basket of phrases to plaster over the darlings' troubles. I waited. I knew that, clever or not, Edward had racked up an impressive string of expulsions, each from a school more expensive and permissive than the last. Crystal, Gilson had said, had survived a famous establishment that provided exemplary training in art and horsemanship and required only a nodding acquaintance with more academic subjects.

"You can't expect children like that to conform," Mrs. Blythe continued airily. "The schools did not provide the challenges they needed. Especially for Edward. He's impatient. Crystal knows how to wait."

"Yet, it is Crystal who appears to be missing."

"Crystal is dramatic. She likes to be noticed; she always has." Mrs. Blythe smiled brightly as though this were a particularly endearing trait. "She always had to be the center of attention, and she succeeded. How she succeeded! She made everything revolve around her, even as a child. Everyone here adored her."

Crystal Blythe sounded like a disagreeable girl.

"Do you think her disappearance is just a bid for attention?"

"Don't be vulgar! Of course not! Crystal was always noticed and loved. Everyone loves Crystal. She's traveling, that's all. She'll come back suddenly and astonish us with something or other." Mrs. Blythe's hands fluttered of their own accord, then dropped limply to her lap. What would cause our astonishment was not defined.

"Is Crystal in the habit of disappearing like this?"

"No, I simply mean — "

"With a boy, perhaps?"

"No! Definitely not! It was a mistake to raise the matter, I can see that. I should never have talked to Berty. You don't understand my children, Miss Peters."

I would have been delighted to end my acquaintance with the Blythes right then, but I persisted. "Mrs. Blythe, your daughter does something that you say is quite unlike her, yet you don't wish to have the matter investigated. From what I understand, I agree that I'm not the right person for this. You should be in contact with the Paris police."

"That's out of the question. I have made that clear to Edward. Crystal would never forgive me. Never!" She seemed genuinely agitated.

"Is it Crystal you're worried about — or old Mrs. Blythe?"

"Crystal — and Edward, too." Mrs. Blythe looked furtive and harassed. "My mother-in-law hates me. She's already tied up the children's money in trusts. There are all sorts of restrictions. I don't know how she expects the children to live as it is. With a scandal, I don't know what she would do."

"What happens to the money if the old lady decides against your son and daughter? The local cat and dog home?"

"Missionaries," Mrs. Blythe whispered in a voice of dread, "missionaries and historic preservation."

"Williamsburg is nice."

"It's no joking matter, Miss Peters. My children's whole future depends on her. They're unworldly. They don't understand the consequences — artists never do. But Crystal must be found, and she and Edward must return home. At once."

"All right." It must have been hard to be caught between an idolized child and all those shares of oil stock.

"I was very worried at first. Anything could have happened. Crystal is fearless, you know. She isn't afraid of anyone, and some of her friends . . ." Mrs. Blythe's voice trailed off. "Then Edward got a letter from her, and I thought everything would be fine."

"When did the letter arrive?"

"About a week after she disappeared. She said she had gotten bored with the university and had gone to Normandy. She needed time to write." I recognized another of Mrs. Blythe's incantations. Nothing could be the matter with a girl who needed time to write. Not much. I imagined the writing was handsome, muscular, and broke.

"Are you sure it was from Crystal?"

Mrs. Blythe hesitated. "It was typed, but that wasn't unusual. Well, I believed it was. Edward said so. He sent the letter on to me."

"Could I read this letter?"

"I threw it out."

"Threw it out?"

"I didn't know it would be important," she replied querulously. "It wouldn't have helped you, anyway. It was all about writing. The inner life."

Crystal and Edward had their mother figured out very nicely.

"But she didn't write again, and Grandmother Blythe asked about her, and I, I began to wonder."

"To wonder what?"

"They're so creative, you understand, everything's a drama with them. They're not ordinary children. Is that the right way to put it? I don't mean abnormal or anything horrid, just unusual, charming, and imaginative. They get caught up in what they're doing, and sometimes they forget it's a game. Things can get out of hand, like the time Edward — " She broke off. "We won't go into ancient history. You'll know what

I mean when you meet Edward. They're so much alike that you'll understand Crystal, too. You'll know how exceptional they are right away."

"You're suggesting that Crystal's disappearance is a prank? You're sure of that?"

"Not a prank, but they're so dramatic. They tend to do things, harmless things, for effect."

"But you don't think your daughter has been hurt in any way? You're not alarmed for her safety?"

Mrs. Blythe looked uncertain.

"If you're sure she isn't in danger, I'd advise you to order Edward home. Cut off his money, and send someone he trusts to bring him home immediately."

"No, no, we can't do that. That's Berty's idea, but no, you'll need Edward there. Nobody knows his sister as he does."

"Edward won't come back, you mean."

"Don't be cruel. Of course, he'd come back! But not without Crystal. They're inseparable, you see. Just in case we're wrong, he has to be there."

"All right, Mrs. Blythe." Obviously, she had no control over her son. "But since there is a possibility that Crystal and Edward are simply indulging their imaginations, I'd appreciate it if you wouldn't let Edward know I'm coming. That's important. And please contact me if anything else happens: if he writes to you again, anything like that."

She agreed reluctantly and gave me some snapshots of Edward and Crystal. Then she began repeating everything she'd said about the young Blythes' virtues, as if fearful I might remain unconvinced. Finally, I left. As I crossed the drive to my car a groom appeared, leading a fine chestnut hunter.

"Good afternoon."

"Afternoon, miss."

I remembered the snapshots and asked, "Is that Crystal's horse? Her mother was just showing me some pictures."

"No, that would have been Eagle she was on in them. Good gelding, he was. Her cousin has him now. Too slow for Miss Crystal."

"Is she a good rider?"

"The best. Both of them are, her and her brother. It's like everything else with them, though."

"Oh, how's that?"

"Miss Crystal got the nerves. Take a horse over anything."

The animal shifted its feet and shook its head impatiently.

"Easy there, fellow. Good day, miss."

He led the animal down an extension of the drive toward the stables, and I thought that it must be hard work being Crystal Blythe's twin brother.

If I had been feeling smart, I would have examined that idea. I wasn't feeling smart. I was feeling hot, tired, dusty, and quite disinterested in the Blythe darlings. The next day, while I sat waiting for Mademoiselle Chantell in a chicly frigid restaurant, my main concern was to conclude the interview as quickly as possible. I had things to do in Washington.

"Miss Peters?"

The voice was stern, precise, and foreign. It belonged to a tall, lean woman wearing an elegant black hat and gloves despite the sultry New York heat. Mademoiselle Chantell was somewhere in her fifties. She had a bony face stamped with an excess of character, a long, thin nose, and dark hooded eyes under high-flying arched brows. Her black hair was streaked with gray and pulled back severely. A lifetime of upholding standards had left its mark: her posture was exemplary, her demeanor regal. She could have passed for a duchess.

"How do you do, Mademoiselle Chantell. It was good of you to come."

"I believed it was my duty," she said as she sat down, adding with a faint smile, "the food here is quite satisfactory. Do you know French food? No? Permit me to order for you. Their chef is erratic."

I nodded, and she took out a small pair of glasses, balanced them at the midpoint of her nose, and examined the menu. After a few minutes she summoned the waiter and the sommelier and carried on an extended conversation.

"Now, Miss Peters," she said when they were dismissed, "what is it that you do?"

"I work for New World Oil Corporation. Mr. Blythe was on our Board of Directors. I head the department that investigates future executive personnel and researches the financial status of our competitors."

"And are you based here in the city?"

"No, I'm in the Washington office."

Her eyebrows arched higher. "I see."

"I had to come up to consult with Mrs. Blythe."

"Mrs. Blythe was more than usually vague about you. I would be pleased if you would enlighten me about your business with Crystal. Is she in some difficulty?"

"So far, Crystal is causing the Blythes difficulties. I hope that's as far as it goes, but I honestly know very little about her or about what is going on."

"She is a young woman with great capacities — in every direction," Mademoiselle Chantell responded dryly.

"Mrs. Blythe said something of that sort."

"In spite of her mother's exaggerations, Crystal *is* able and intelligent. Exceedingly so."

"You were with the Blythes nearly eleven years. Tell me, did the children strike you as normal, stable youngsters?"

"I am not, Miss Peters, of the Freudian persuasion."

"I did not suspect you were."

She gave an ironic laugh. "You will understand then when I say that there are no 'normal' children. Edward and Crystal are definitely unusual. They are very gifted, and they have had an unusual life."

"Unusual in what way?"

"You have met Mrs. Blythe."

"Yes, I have. Was she always so — "

"She was always a foolish woman. After her husband's death, she became unable to direct her children's lives. I stayed with them even after they went to school. I don't wish to criticize her: she was ridiculously sheltered, first by her parents, then by her husband. She was raised to be nothing at all, Miss Peters, and her upbringing was overwhelmingly successful."

"She seems to dote on her children."

"Certainly. The idea of them she liked — in the abstract."

"And what about you? Did you like them?"

"They could be enchanting."

That left a lot of latitude.

"Has Crystal been in touch with you lately?"

"No, she has not. Are you looking for her, Miss Peters?"

"After a fashion. Do you have any idea where she might go if she wanted to avoid her family?"

"Crystal and Edward had few friends. They lived like gypsies. We used to move — six in staff, the children, myself, and Mrs. Blythe — every month or so. From one of their houses to the other; Mrs. Blythe simply could not settle. Texas to Virginia to Connecticut to Maine. Poor Edward. How he hated Maine."

"Why was that?"

"The water. We were right on the coast, just above Bar Harbor. I'm surprised she didn't mention that, but then, you were discussing Crystal."

"She made some remark about his not liking boats."

"He is the only child I ever tutored who could not learn to swim. It wasn't the typical fear of water; that's quite easily overcome with patience. It was, and probably has remained, sheer terror. I often wondered about the reason. Crystal swam beautifully, but in everything else except riding Edward was the superior athlete. Something must have happened before I came, but what, I don't know. With families like the Blythes . . ."

"Yes?"

"It's often hard to get information. Too much turnover in the staff." Her long face grew even longer in disapproval.

"I can imagine. What about their schools?"

"School came rather late in their development. They were over twelve. Until then, I educated them. I don't know who their friends are now. They were always alone."

"That presents a complication."

"More than one, I assure you."
"Mrs. Blythe said the children are extremely talented. How much is she exaggerating?"
"The children are talented. Crystal is highly intelligent. They used to perform plays that were quite remarkable. That is where Edward shone. He could make himself whatever he wished. His dramatic abilities were striking; he acted with absolute conviction. Remarkable, both of them. But they were unwilling to perfect their gifts. They were not honest in that sense."
Mademoiselle Chantell must have been a rather frightening tutor.
"They were young," I suggested.
"Age is not the issue," she replied firmly. "Their mother thought that also. It was one reason I could not remain. On that I could not compromise."
I was surprised that Mrs. Blythe had endured so forceful a personality for eleven years.
"Minds like that," she continued, "require discipline. If they are not strong they are dangerous, Miss Peters." The long, heavy lids drooped over her eyes, and she folded her napkin to signal that the interview was over. "A satisfactory meal, I think."
"Yes, it was delicious."
"Will you be seeing Edward?"
"I plan to. He is needed at home, too, and I am hoping that he will have some information about his sister."
"Give my love to him, but don't take what he says uncritically. Edward's imagination sometimes gets in the way of strict truth."
"I'll remember that. Could you suggest anyone else I might talk to about Crystal?"
"She perhaps met some girls at school?"
"A Sue Almon. Did you know her?"
Mademoiselle Chantell shook her head. "She was mentioned, that's all."
"Any boyfriends you know of?"

"I heard there was a difficulty her last year in school, but I am unclear as to the exact circumstances. To say more would be simply to repeat gossip."

I thanked her for her help and paid the bill. Mademoiselle Chantell had not skimped on our wine.

"They were, as young children, so charming," she said as we started to leave. "I remember in the summer in Connecticut they used to light candles on the terrace by the pond and do little programs — music or recitations or plays. Puppets. They had puppets, too. There was such material there." She held out her hand. "Good day, Miss Peters. You will find the Blythes . . . interesting, I am sure."

"Interesting," *le mot juste*. When Harry asked me how my inquiries were coming, I said, "Interesting."

"Interesting? Do you realize," he asked with mock solemnity, "that you have been off for four days on a series of expensive junkets to New York, Virginia, and darkest Connecticut and all you can say is 'interesting'?"

I gave him a brief account of my meetings with Mrs. Blythe and her retainers, ending with school friend Sue Almon's brother, who assured me that Crystal was a bit wild but "a helluva girl."

"I don't think this will be so hard," Harry remarked when I finished.

"No?"

"Not at all. Just locate a troupe of good-looking young actors who travel around putting on plays and living artistic lives."

"Sounds to me as though she's been kidnapped by the gypsies."

"No, that's outdated. There was a big fad for that once, but it's passé now."

"No chance then. Mrs. Blythe assured me that Crystal's the epitome of good taste."

"I'm glad to hear that," he replied. "Traveling actors, that's the thing."

"I thought they were rather out of style, too."

Harry shrugged. "Well, a politician, or a rock singer, or a

nightclub pianist — that's a bit seedy, though, isn't it?"

"Chauvinistic, too. Maybe she ran away on her own."

"Bottom of the Seine, maybe."

"I don't think so, somehow — unless someone dumped her in. If she's anything like her mother, I can see how it could happen."

"Don't suggest that until we've been there a while. I've got a lot I want to see, then there's the cinémathèque, and I've been thinking about a trip to Colmar."

"Don't drag the river until we've seen the altarpiece?"

"Right."

"That's a sound plan," I said. "And now, I've got to pack. I have a meeting with some French oil people the day after we get in, so we'd better make the plane."

# Chapter 3

WE MET ANTOINE FERMINE in Paris. Or, to be precise, Antoine Fermine met us, complete with greetings from the New World people in France, various projects of his own, and, more practically, a car. I spotted him as soon as we approached the Air France desk. A neat, well-built fellow with wire-rimmed glasses and little, shiny brown eyes, he was leaning against the counter, pestering one of the women employees. He wore a good American suit, his hair was cut short, and he welcomed us with a cheerful, open smile. He was so precisely what delights an oil company executive that I was prepared to dislike him immediately.

"Miss Peters? Mr. Radford?"

"That's right. You must be from New World Oil."

"Antoine Fermine. Call me Tony. It sounds better in English, don't you think?" We shook hands; he grabbed our luggage and assured us that everything was in order. Had we had a good trip? Wonderful weather. The hotel was excellent. The company liked things first rate, he confided, and the car was this way. Antoine shepherded us through Charles de Gaulle with the domineering cheerfulness of a professional tour guide, which, it appeared, he was. Before we reached the parking lot, he had already offered us a guided tour of the city, a round of nightclubs, a day at the races, and a fancy dinner. When we demurred, he blushed and looked speculative, as though trying to discover what outré pleasures this pair of Americans had in mind. It was perfectly clear that he had no idea why we needed him.

We left the airport via a maze of concrete ramps and sped across the modern industrial section that surrounds Paris. With the hot wind blowing in the windows, we might have been in

New Jersey, except for the sparse fields and the old stone and stucco houses clinging with their tiny gardens to the very edges of the highway.

"I'm half American, you know," Antoine said. I didn't respond; the swaying car was giving me a headache. "Ever been to the States?" Harry asked politely. People who can sleep on planes have all the advantages in a personality contest.

"Sure have. I went to high school there and then spent two years at Yale. That was enough. I came back here and stayed with Mother for a while. I needed to get out into the real world."

"Into New World, you mean?"

Tony laughed pleasantly. "No, no, nothing so established. Paris-by-Night Tours. That was all I could get. My father was mad at me for leaving Yale, so I got no help from him. I know every joint in town. Too much air for you, Miss Peters?"

"No, that's fine."

"Then T-shirts. I branched out, just at the right time, you could say. Paris souvenir T-shirts. The coming thing over here."

"Where did you sell them?" I asked, making an effort to sound interested.

"Oh, round and about. It was a shoestring operation at first, but I did all right on it. Then my father relented and introduced me to some guys at New World."

"Very convenient."

"It's a fun job. But it's all a matter of attitude, don't you agree? I didn't mind selling souvenirs, either."

Harry asked him about the process of printing shirts and about the newer art galleries. As they talked, the city emerged from its suburbs, towers, domes, and spires soaring above broad avenues and parks. Sunlight swam through the leaves of the dusty chestnut trees, warmed the gray stone buildings, and sparkled on the Seine and on the gold-trimmed bridges arching its waters. The ubiquitous mopeds sputtered alongside us, and spidery wood and metal chairs clustered under bright awnings and umbrellas at every corner café. Everything seemed charming: infinitely better than a working day in Washington. When Antoine pulled up at a small hotel just off the Champs-Élysées, I told him he could have the rest of the day off.

"Jet lag, huh? Well, I'll be here first thing tomorrow. Is there anything you need? Anything special from the hotel? That's what I'm here for, you know." His bright eyes darted like fish behind his round glasses.

"Come at one tomorrow. That will be soon enough. We'll discuss what I want done then."

"Oh," he said, surprised. "O.K., anything you want. I can always find something to do in the meantime." He repeated directions to Harry, consulted with the concierge, and led us to a pair of fine large rooms with striped wallpaper and flowered curtains.

"He's certainly enthusiastic," Harry said when Antoine left.

"An enthusiastic idiot."

"Oh, he's just a kid. He knows all the galleries, though."

"You can have him. I don't think he could find a lost dog. I ask Gilson to get me someone fluent and competent and whom does he send? A Joe College who wants to take us on a tour of the strip joints."

"Well," Harry said reasonably, "he probably wasn't told he's to help look for a stockholder's daughter."

"No, I suppose not, but he's hardly going to advance the process."

"So much the better."

I unpacked my suitcase while Harry peered out the windows, checked his maps, and generated a lot of restless anticipation.

"I'll tell you what," he said, "let's take today off. We can take a boat on the river. It'll be cooler there. Then we'll have a super dinner and go to bed early. You can get rid of Tony in the morning if you're sure he won't do."

"All right, let's see the sights."

"This way to the Seine."

"Oh, wait a minute. How do you say 'safe' in French, the kind you lock up?"

"*Cache*, I think. Where are you going with that?" he asked, pointing to my attaché case.

"New World's papers. Rule number one: never leave them lying around."

"What about the pictures in your suitcase?"

"They'll be all right. I don't think school photos will tempt anyone."

*

It was hot, almost as warm as D.C., and contrary to Harry's expectations, the river was no improvement. We sat on the blazing deck of a pleasure boat and were gently broiled by the sun reflected from the water and refracted through the surrounding glass. Over our pyre, a disembodied voice extolled the riverside beauties in three languages. I admired them sincerely and admired even more the shaded quais where fishermen and lovers drowsed. Harry, of course, with true artistic toughness, was beyond discomfort; he paced from one side of the vessel to the other, snapping the green Île de la Cité and Notre-Dame and this king's bridge and that philosopher's house and all those young men sunbathing in their microscopic swim trunks. Afterward, we refreshed ourselves with a warm, fizzy concoction and wandered listlessly over the white sand in the park. I didn't revive until the sun dipped behind the Arc de Triomphe, cast its dusty golden shafts down the Champs-Élysées, and left our café table in shadow.

"How do you feel?" Harry asked with belated solicitude.

"As if I'd crossed the Alps with Hannibal. You never told me you were supertourist."

"Only here. Paris brings back happy memories."

I hoped I'd have some of those. Then the waiter brought the antidote for tourism: bowls of glorious French soup. I decided I'd survive.

"The last time I was here, I made a lot of drawings and watercolors of the area along the Seine, the bird market, the flower market — you couldn't see them from the boat, they're behind Notre-Dame. Some of those quais, some of the bridges at dusk; Paris has a beautiful blue twilight." He watched the strollers promenading and scribbled on his napkin. "That was after I came back from Vietnam."

Nineteen sixty-four or sixty-five, I thought. Harry never talked about Vietnam.

"I needed a change," he added simply.

The scribbles resolved themselves into the umbrellas and tables of a sidewalk café.

"Glad you now have a patron at New World Oil?"

He waved at the magnificent avenue and the clear golden light flooding through its western gateway, the Arc de Triomphe.

"Who wouldn't be?"

As we walked toward the Louvre after dinner, I began to agree. The Tuileries Gardens were lit for the ballet, and the chestnut trees wore chokers of round yellow bulbs that lit marble arms and nymphs' feet and the dark flowers bedded in their shadows. At the head of the garden, the obelisk stretched between the whirlpool of Concorde traffic and the high curve of night, while chunks of heroic statuary and wonderful iron lamps looked on like Gallic trolls. I found it easy to lose the paranoia essential for hunting money and heiresses, and I didn't recover it until I stepped out of the shower between our rooms.

"Anna, were you looking in my suitcase?"

"No, why?"

"Someone's been through my stuff."

Harry has no paranoia at all, so I wrapped myself in a towel and had a look.

"Missing anything?"

"No. Maybe it was just a nosy chambermaid."

I shook my head. I was glad I had put my New World papers in the hotel safe. Most of the material on Crystal was there, too. Everything except the pictures. They were still in my suitcase, but I was sure they had been rearranged.

"You're dressed, Harry. Ask if anyone came looking for us today, would you?"

"But don't mention that someone's been in our luggage?"

"No, if you don't mind. I don't want it to get back to our friend Tony."

"That's very considerate of you," he said dryly and winked.

I put on my robe and admired the stars from the fire escape at the end of the hall. The metal stairs ended about six feet from the ground, not too far for someone athletic.

"You have hidden talents, too," Harry said when he returned. "A young man asked for you this afternoon."

"Surprise, surprise."

"He did not, of course, monsieur, go up to your room."

"Not by the front stairs, anyway."

"Unfortunately, monsieur, I was not on duty at the time," Harry continued with appropriate gestures. "He should have left a note."

"That's where he's wrong," I said. "Our visitor has left a message. He's told us that he knows why we're here. Damn! I should have taken your advice about the pictures."

"That was silly of you, but you can make up for it."

"How?"

"Take the advice I'm going to give you now," he said, switching off the overhead light. "Think about your heiress tomorrow, but concentrate on me tonight."

The sky was an exquisite shade of purple, and the cars and mopeds made a soft rushing sound. I took his advice, but I woke with the thought that Tony Fermine might not be as naïve as he appeared.

\*

I kept my appointment the next morning with Monsieur Morret, the director of a large petrochemical firm that held important New World contracts. He greeted me in a room that wouldn't have embarrassed Marie Antoinette. The walls were covered with mirrors, and whatever wasn't mirrored had been carved and gilded. Three large and beautiful tapestries with overweight ladies and half-armored gentlemen hung in stately file, and the gilt furniture deposed on the gleaming parquetry was ornate and silk-cushioned. One felt underdressed without a wig, crinolines, ostrich feathers, and an extravagance of satin.

"Ah, *bonjour,* Mademoiselle Peters. *Enchanté. Merci, merci.* How nice of you to bring us this *personnellement.* It was too kind of Monsieur Gilson. How is my good friend Bertrand? I haven't seen him in several years."

I stumbled through the obligatory greetings *en français,* assuring him I was delighted to be of assistance and very pleased to meet him. Then I lapsed gratefully back into English, feeling as though I'd completed a tricky exam.

Morret beamed and ordered coffee. He was a tall, substantial man with a wide girth and narrow shoulders like the actor Philippe Noiret, and he had a long, wasted face with an aquiline nose and black eyes. He moved with ponderous and courtly assurance, and he waited patiently until his secretary, a palid young man with a well-bred, underfed look brought us coffee and croissants.

"Bertrand mentioned that you are in research."

"That's right. We work with the personnel department, evaluating prospective executives, as well as in financial research."

"An interesting combination," he remarked and went on to discuss personnel practices in general. His English was idiosyncratic but fluent, and from the occasional hesitations in his conversation, I got the impression that he was hinting at something. "Please tell my friend Bertrand how much we appreciate these security reports. Your company, *malheureusement,* has had a need for such precautions. We also are coming to see their importance."

"Yes, I'm sure that after Metz you've given more thought to security policies." A lot of lives were lost when the oil refinery at Metz was bombed by terrorists in August 1976.

"To be sure," Monsieur Morret replied. "Yes, we, the oil industry in France, have begun certain investigations on our own. You might find this interesting, Mademoiselle Peters. We have computerized a profile of the type of personality who is involved in terrorist activities. With the help of the Sûreté, we have obtained information on a number of, ah, dangerous — no — going to be — "

"Potentially?"

"Yes, potentially dangerous individuals. We are using our printout to predict events, perhaps, and to screen employees. Would you like to meet the programmer who is working with this data?"

"Yes, I would. I'm sure it would be most interesting."

"*Bon.* I will introduce you to Albert," he said.

I was ready to leave, but Monsieur Morret remained seated and gazed through the handsome silk drapes toward the Champs-Élysées. I wondered what it was he wanted to say.

"I hope you will remember my willingness to assist you, Mademoiselle Peters," he said after a moment. "I have valuable contacts not ordinarily available to visiting foreigners. Should you need my assistance, I assure you that everything will be handled with care."

"Thank you, Monsieur Morret, but I'm here for a holiday. The only thing I'm doing for the company is calling on a few of Mr. Gilson's old friends."

"Of course, of course, Mademoiselle Peters," he replied smoothly. "But for the future, who knows when we might discover mutually valuable information?"

I agreed that that was a possibility, toured computer headquarters, and within an hour was walking back to the hotel through the clear Parisian sunshine. The trip no longer felt so much like a vacation. Monsieur Morret was the second person to be more curious than he ought to be about my trip to Paris, and I didn't like it. As for the "mutually valuable information" I might dig up, I appreciated that even less.

*

Antoine was relaxing against the desk when I came downstairs. "How are you feeling today, Miss Peters?" he asked cheerfully. "You don't mind if I call you Anna, do you?"

"Not at all," I said. When we were outside the hotel, I suggested that we find somewhere to sit and talk.

"There's a tabac around the corner," he said. Then he dropped his voice to add: "I'm alert to the security implications."

"The what?"

"Oh, it's O.K.," he said calmly and confidently, "now that we're alone, that is. I don't think that we need pretend I'm your guide, do you?"

"Just what were you told by the New World people?"

"Everything. We are to find Crystal Blythe, without tipping off the police or any other agency that might be interested," he whispered. He scanned the half-empty tables of the tabac like a B-movie conspirator, "and we are to use the utmost discretion."

Someone had talked too much at New World Oil, but I let it pass. "Yes," I said, deciding to make the best of a bad situation, "we are to make inquiries. I will be a relative of Crystal's, and you are a friend who is helping me. Does that sound too implausible?"

"Oh, not at all," he replied quickly. "You don't sound like a rich American, but they won't know that over here."

"No, I don't suppose so. If you understand what we're doing, why did we have that little charade the other day?"

"Oh," he answered with great seriousness, "with Mr. Radford there — "

"Harry is aware of the purpose of the trip. He's not responsible for finding Crystal, but he knows why I'm here."

"Do you think that's wise? It is important that — "

"I think, Tony, that we will get along better if you let me make the decisions and if you keep most of your opinions to yourself." Despite his air of wholesome good cheer, there was something pedantic about Tony Fermine.

"All right," he said stiffly, "but I know how serious this could be. I'm not sure you realize how full of dangerous radicals this city is. When I left Yale, I thought I'd left all that behind. There are Reds of every stripe here — Marxists, Leninists, Maoists — believe me, this is some place."

"Ideological purity was never my strong point. I think it would be better if you just translate what I tell you and never mind the political repercussions. Now, I am Crystal's distant but very distressed Aunt Anna. You may be whomever you wish, but keep Tony as your first name."

He looked cross, but said nothing. I showed him Crystal's last address. "Know where this is?"

"Of course."

"Well, where is it?"

"Just off the Luxembourg Gardens, near the Sorbonne. A lot of students live in that area."

"Right. That's where Crystal was living when she disappeared. The rent has been paid, so the apartment is still as she left it — or so I'm told. We're going to make anxious inquiries of the concierge. Then we are going to search the room carefully."

He nodded.

"Let me talk to the concierge first. When my French gives out, I will become very upset. If the concierge is difficult, I may even manage to shed a few tears. I expect you to be very eloquent and protective, and here is two hundred francs, if something more substantial is required. Hold on to whatever is left and keep an accounting. It's all on expenses."

Tony brightened visibly at the prospect of disguise, bribery, and investigation. Lord knows who he thought would be lurking in the wings, but he seemed ready to play his part.

"Don't worry, Anna," he said, "we'll find Crystal one way or the other."

I thought about the fire escape to our room. "Good," I replied.

# Chapter 4

THE BROAD SIDEWALKS of the Boulevard Saint-Michel have tempted Latin Quarter shopkeepers to an ebullient expansion. Awnings and porches, racks and frames, and bins of merchandise sprawl from storefront to curbside, while books, posters, belts, blouses, and souvenirs are hung on stands or flung into large, untidy piles. Wherever the merchants have hesitated, slender Africans have spread blankets, offering an identical line of letter openers, ebony elephants, fertility charms, bracelets, and buffalo-hide safari hats, all imported from Taiwan and Korea. A few lethargic art students complete the throng, with tired pastel portraits defying all laws of anatomy.

Past this bazaar flows a polyglot stream of students, vendors, and tourists in sandals and jeans and loose shirts of ethnic inspiration. Tony pushed through the tide with the air of a man who knew his surroundings well.

"Turn here," he said finally. "It can't be more than a block."

We walked down a clean, narrow side street, past a small patisserie, to a large building with a cobblestone courtyard. The liquid music of the Near East dripped monotonously from its upper reaches, and just inside the archway, a large family of Indians stood, consulting their green Michelin. At the rear of the courtyard was an entrance to a small dark lobby that doubled as a breakfast room. Dishes rattled in the interior, and an argument ensued, half in French and half in Spanish. Tony leaned on the desk and rang the bell while I removed my dark glasses and attempted to look anxious. Two women hurried down the corridor, a tall, swarthy waitress carrying a tray of dishes like a battering ram, and a small, red-haired shrew who looked us up and down and announced: *"Pas de chambres."*

Tony smoothed his jacket and, with many gestures and reassuring nods toward his unhappy relative, established our complete probity. I stammered that I was Crystal Blythe's aunt. The concierge turned her sharp eyes in my direction and listened while I described the worries of Crystal's *pauvre mama* in my uncertain French. She expressed sympathy, but said, *"Mademoiselle, c'est impossible,"* a statement she elaborated upon to Tony with considerably more force.

"She says she doesn't want any trouble."

"I understand. Tell her I've come all the way from the States. Say Crystal's grandmother is ill."

This was faithfully translated. There were references to the police.

"It's very urgent," I said. Tony repeated this, adding hints as to the form our gratitude might take.

The woman wavered, but suggested reporting our names to the local authorities. I've never been crazy about the police, so I grabbed the woman's arm and cried, "The police! What's happened to Crystal?" Obviously Aunt Anna was distraught. As the coup de grâce, I buried my face in my hands and turned toward the door just slowly enough to see Tony bring out a hundred-franc note. Within minutes we were clanking toward the fifth floor in a lacy wrought-iron elevator. The concierge opened Crystal's door, and I remembered to mutter something about my poor niece and sink weakly onto the bed. The concierge offered a cup of tea.

*"Merci, madame. Thé, s'il vous plaît,"* I responded as Tony started to decline.

"I'll come down and get it," he told the woman with some irritation, ushering her out and closing the door behind him. I stood up and looked around. It was a wide, airy room with two pairs of windows opening onto tiny railed balconies. From there I had an excellent view of the street below, of the tabac on the corner and of the red-robed youth doing calisthenics in the dormer room over the café. The walls were papered an innocuous yellow, but with the white iron bed, the fireplace flanked with bookshelves, a good rug, and white curtains, it was a pleasant place. A table stood in one corner with a sink and a hot plate next to it, and the door opposite led to a full bathroom. Crystal's affectation of student life hadn't brought any real changes to her existence. An elevator, breakfast in her room, maid service, and good plumbing did not exactly add up to deprivation; neither did the oriental rug by the bed nor the pretty antique chest.

Lucky girl, I thought, as I started on the closets. Crystal had abandoned a nice wardrobe, not practical but expensive and attractive. Her muddled mom was right about one thing: the girl had good taste — evening dresses and hostess skirts, three pairs of riding breeches, several hacking jackets, and a black gabardine number with a green velvet collar for formal equestrienne wear. There were riding boots and flimsy heels but neither casual shoes nor clothes, and from the abundance of empty hangers, I suspected that Crystal had decamped with more than the clothes on her back. I shut the closet and opened the top drawer of her bureau. She'd left behind some underwear and a black leather jewelry box that rattled when I shook it. I was rummaging through my bag for a paper clip when Tony returned, bearing a slopping cup of tea.

"Do you have a paper clip — a piece of wire or anything like that?"

"I think so." He set the cup down and fumbled in his pocket. "This do?"

"Probably. Here, see if you can get this open," I said, handing him the box.

"Should we? I don't think I — "

"We don't have much time, so give it a try. Didn't the CIA teach you anything?"

"What do you mean?" he asked in amazement. When he was angry, that nice open face closed up tight and hard. It was the sort of face that sold you groceries on Monday and brought the mob to see you on Saturday night.

"Joke, Tony. Joke."

He started to say something, then began to fiddle with the box. I counted the cashmere sweaters stuffed negligently into the second drawer. He pried the lock and, taking a quick look inside, set the box on the bureau and stalked to the closet. I expected some of his usual chatter, but he was too angry. That was worth noting. Either he had an unusually poor sense of humor or, unwittingly, I had been right on target.

There was a printed soccer schedule stuck between the drawers, but the bureau held nothing of interest. I looked at her jewelry: a handful of costume pieces and modest antiques, not valuable, but not exactly what you'd pin on a sweatshirt, either. I admired a garnet bracelet and an ostentatious Chinese necklace.

"Nothing here," Tony said.

"No, I imagine her good jewelry is in a safe-deposit box. This is interesting, though."

"That's not worth anything. See, it's chipped."

The small pendant was a sandwich of onyx and crystal engraved with the figure of a monkey sitting in a bamboo thicket. It must have been a favorite trinket: in addition to the chipped edges and the tarnished chain, a childish hand had scratched "Crystal B." on the back. I returned it to the box.

"I don't think there's anything here," Tony repeated, and he outlined a plan for questioning the neighbors.

"Later," I said and went to examine the bookcases, which had puzzled me from the first. People usually dislike empty shelves and fill them up with knickknacks. Crystal's bookcases were completely bare. I stood on a chair to examine the top shelves. The front of each was clean, but the back was very dusty. I looked at the lower shelves again and then checked the bathroom. A search there had confirmed both my opinion of the management's housekeeping and my initial supposition about Crystal's particular design for living when the concierge knocked on the door. Tony let her in, and I decided to come straight to the point: *"Où est les livres?"*

Although the concierge was startled, she shook her head stubbornly: there had never been any books.

*"Oui, plus des livres."* I pointed to the shelves.

*"Non, non, mademoiselle."* She went over to the shelves and began speaking rapidly. Tony translated: "She says Crystal had

no books. The shelves have been empty all this time. You can see how clean they are. No one has touched any of Mademoiselle Blythe's possessions."

I ignored this defense of the establishment's integrity and pointed to the chair in front of the bookcase. "Tell her to look at the top shelves. *Le plus haut.*"

After indignant protests, the concierge ascended. Immediately we received an outburst, which needed no translation, concerning the lazy, good-for-nothing chambermaid.

I nodded sympathetically and asked where Crystal's boyfriend was. More denials. I led the way to the bathroom and asked whether the large wicker laundry basket was theirs or Crystal's. It was Crystal's. I moved it away from the wall and fished up a wilted athletic supporter. The concierge shrugged. I handed her my other find, the soccer schedule, and signaled to Tony to give her more money. Adjourning to the bedroom, we spent more than we'd bargained and learned less than we'd hoped.

According to the concierge, Crystal's friend visited frequently. She believed he was a student, since he seemed to have neither money nor a job. Unfortunately, she couldn't tell us his full name. Crystal referred to him only as "Gaby."

"Gabriel?" I asked.

She nodded. Tony translated: "Probably. He was a quiet boy — tall, green eyes, brown hair."

"French?"

"Yes, but not Parisian. Alsatian, perhaps."

"Were they his books?"

"She thinks so, because Mademoiselle did not appear to be a reader."

That was my impression, too. "What sort of books were they?"

"She doesn't know. She had better things to do than to read her tenant's books."

I told Tony to assure her that only my deep concern for Crystal made me persistent. This was a fiction she didn't believe but appreciated, and we exchanged expressions of anxiety. I asked if the man had come for his books. She hesitated, began to say yes, changed to no, and then settled into a stony silence that cost another hundred francs to break. "Another young man, a friend of Gaby's and Crystal's, moved the books," Tony interpreted. The concierge shrugged as if to indicate no one could object. I asked when this had happened.

"Several days after Crystal left."

"I think it's odd that a conscientious woman like yourself would let a stranger take books from a tenant's room."

Tony repeated this in French, but the concierge offered no explanation. I opened my bag and showed her a photograph. *"Est-ce que cet homme?"*

Tony craned his neck to see, but showed no sign of surprise or recognition. The concierge sighed unhappily. *"Oui, cet homme."*

"Edward Blythe," I said.

She nodded resignedly.

We spent a few more minutes discussing where we might find friends of the mysterious Gaby's, but I was convinced that the concierge had divulged all she knew. I asked her to say nothing to Edward if he should return; she agreed, and we left.

Outside, the boulevard was shady, and it was pleasant to walk idly past the shops and restaurants that lined the long slope to the Luxembourg. We entered the park, crossed the grove of chestnut trees, and sat on a bench overlooking the pond and the circular walk with its balustrade garlanded with oleander. I was annoyed with Crystal Blythe. Finding her was going to be a tedious process, and instead of roaming galleries and parks with Harry, I would be stuck working with Tony Fermine. That was a dreary prospect.

"Well," I said, interrupting his scrutiny of a pair of pretty strollers, "what do you suggest?"

"Find the boyfriend."

"Or find out about him. We can ask around the neighborhood and around the Sorbonne, and we can check the bookstores. What do you say?"

"The Sorbonne is immense. Unless we know his last name or

his field it'll be almost impossible. I think the people in the neighborhood might know more, and I could easily check that out."

"So you suggested. What bothers me are the books."

"Maybe that was just coincidence, or he might have wanted to get rid of Gaby's stuff for spite or something."

"No, I don't think so. I don't suppose they were worth anything — that concierge would have known to the last centime if they had been — so it had to be for some other reason. This is the quarter for bookstores, isn't it?"

"Sure, but there are dozens."

"Yes, but let's assume this guy's a student. That means scholarly books, cheap, used books."

"Maybe, but that's the specialty here." Tony was skeptical.

"There has to be something about them, something that would identify him unmistakably, otherwise why would Edward have bothered to remove them?"

"It would be easier to run down Edward and ask him point blank."

That was true, but the obvious means of proceeding aren't always the best, especially when you're dealing with a theatrical, unreliable person like Edward. Evidently honesty wasn't his long suit, and since even his mother suspected he might be lying about Crystal's disappearance, it would be better to know what was going on first and visit him later. I didn't bother to explain this to Tony; I outlined another approach.

"O.K.," he shrugged when I'd finished. "That might work."

"And if we can find out, it will be more plausible for you to go inquiring as a fellow medical or literary or whatever student."

He agreed. We began on the boulevard and worked our way to the Seine and back down the side streets. Policemen call this "legwork," and I soon saw why. The pavements made mine ache and turned my feet into two disagreeable appendages. Worse yet, no one recognized Crystal's picture or remembered her friend Gaby. Most people were very pleasant. Yes, they could understand our difficulty in finding where she lived. "A bookstore on the corner" wasn't much to go on in the Latin Quarter, was it? No, they'd remember such a pretty girl, especially if she were a steady customer. Perhaps someone at the university would know about my niece, and so on.

"The stores are going to close soon," Tony said finally.

That sounded marvelous, but I concealed my relief, "We have time for one more. Let's try that little shop and then we'll call it a day."

"It doesn't look promising," he said, and he was right. The dirty window held a clutter of crumbling books and cheap posters, and I could smell the dust from the sidewalk. Inside, the shop was every bit as vile as its windows. I expected the proprietor to be a gnomelike antique, so when a young man in sandals padded out of the backroom, I was suddenly curious. He had a thin olive face and an arrogant, unfriendly manner. Something about him inspired me. I knew his type, and before Tony could begin his spiel, I said, *"Bonjour, monsieur. Mon cousin cherche pour un bon ami qui aime les livres antiques, n'est-ce pas, Antoine?"* and I dug my nails into Tony's arm so hard that he jumped. The shopkeeper gave me a look that could have frozen fish, and Tony began a long dissertation that I made no attempt to follow. Instead, I apologized for my poor French, and, knowing men will ignore a woman to talk to one of their own, I sidled toward the back of the shop.

There were cartons of books on the floor all right: cheap thrillers next to cookbooks, old scientific texts squeezed between forgotten romances. I pushed past a pile of magazines and broken-down quartos to reach the door to the basement. I felt along the wall for the light switch. Tony was still talking, so I descended into the dampness. The room below was set up as a printing shop, with a ditto machine, a small press, and piles of cheaply bound books, pamphlets, and manifestoes, some already packed in cartons. There were yellowing Panther broadsides in English, various Maoist tracts, anti-Zionist propaganda, French material on Vietnam, and a selection of Cuban pamphlets. They didn't seem exactly dangerous, and I was wondering why the phony bookshop upstairs when I heard steps overhead. I ran upstairs, flicked off the light, and closed the door. Then I opened it again, peered into the darkness, and asked *"Toilette?"* innocently, as the proprietor waded through his bibliographical cemetery and began ranting.

"What's the matter?" I asked Tony. "Ask him if he doesn't have a toilet. I don't know what this damn city expects a tourist to do."

Tony repeated this in French, but I was pretty sure the man understood me. I continued to complain about the sanitary facilities until we made our exit.

"Did you learn anything?" I asked.

"Not much, except that the proprietor is either cautious or paranoid. I'm sure he knew whom I was talking about. He kept asking me where I'd met Gaby and how I'd known about the shop. I think it would take a few visits before he'd tell me anything. Why did you go wandering off in search of a john at that moment?"

"Don't be silly. I was checking out his other merchandise. Would it surprise you to learn that the cellar is full of printing equipment and political pamphlets?"

"What kind?"

"Radical leftist. Lots of Maoist stuff."

Tony's eyes lit up, but I prevented another dissertation on the Red Menace. "He's entitled to his opinions. We want to find out more about Gaby, and why Edward thought it worthwhile to get rid of his books.

"Start around the university and see what you can turn up. Quickly, in case our friend in the bookstore is suspicious. I'd avoid the area around Crystal's building, too, unless you can be sure no one will recognize you. Concoct some story, and we'll see what happens — but be sure to leave Crystal out of it."

Tony nodded.

"And don't go dressed like that. If you don't have any French clothes, pick some up at the cheap stores around here."

"All right, all right," he replied with a touch of irritation.

"Good," I said and went to catch the Métro back to the

Champs-Élysées. I was within a block of my hotel when someone called my name. I turned around. He was sitting in the shade with a drink in his hand.

"Well, *bonjour,* Miss Peters," said Edward Blythe.

# Chapter 5

Edward looked exactly like the stunning photographs in his mother's album. He was tall and slim, with golden skin, blond hair, and indigo eyes, poised, it seemed to me, with supreme assurance on that unsteady bridge between youth and manhood. He had the chiseled features, high cheekbones, and fine hands that ladies sigh for in fluffy romances, but his unsettling beauty lay elsewhere, in the grace of his movements. He was the most attractive man I'd ever seen. That was nice. He'd recognized me instantly. And that wasn't.

"It was good of you to come," he said, extending his hand. "I've been waiting to see you. Sit down. What would you like? Mother always drinks gin on a hot day. What about you?"

"Just a Vitel, please."

Edward smiled. His smile was quick and sly and vanished into the dappled shade.

"I'm glad, that you don't drink gin, that is. You're not nearly so awful as I'd imagined. When mother wrote about a detective — she did tell me, of course. Did you know that?" he asked, and he smiled again boyishly, but his eyes were scarcely innocent.

"It wasn't unexpected. Naturally, she's worried," I said, although I was annoyed.

"Yes, Mother's charming once you acquire a taste for her. I'd imagined a fat alcoholic in a loud suit with a cigar and disgusting habits," he continued. "Thank goodness you came instead."

He had extraordinary eyes, but I'm resistant, at least to such obvious flattery. "Your mother wouldn't have approved of him."

"No, not the fat or the cigar, but then, she's not really in charge, is she?"

"What do you mean by 'in charge'?" His mother's opinion to the contrary, Edward did not seem unworldly.

"You work for New World Oil."

"Your family business."

"There is a difference."

"Some of your dad's old friends wanted to spare your mother a fat man in a nasty suit."

"How kind of them."

"So it seems." We sat and stared at each other. He was pleasant to contemplate and I was in no hurry to talk, especially since it could have been Edward in our rooms instead of Tony.

"It's odd, having a corporation as an uncle," he said after a moment, and the smile reappeared.

"I'm sure it's awkward," I replied. "So are police investigations."

"Yes, I'm not sure we can avoid them much longer. I'm scared, Miss Peters. I haven't wanted to worry Mother, but I'm glad you're here."

I thought about the books he'd moved and wondered. "Suppose you tell me what happened."

For a moment he hesitated, as though genuinely puzzled. "It's a little hard to explain," he began. "My sister and I have lived an unconventional life, I mean different even from people like ourselves. Two years ago we'd had enough. We just wanted to be left alone. We were tired of schools, and they were tired of us. And we were tired of my mother's unending self-pity and crises and hypochondria." His voice trembled with bitterness.

"Was there a quarrel?"

"No, we just left," he replied, calm again. "As you perhaps know, we came into a guaranteed allowance at eighteen, so money was no problem. We moved here. We rented an apartment in the Roule, which I still have. We were very happy."

"Where is the Roule?"

"Near here — the eighth arrondissement."

"Your mother gave me a Latin Quarter address for Crystal. When did she move out?"

"About six months ago. She'd been attending classes at the

Sorbonne. So had I, in fact, although I don't think Mother believed me. She doesn't, you know, not the way she believes Crystal. Well, my sister decided to play at the student life. In other words," he added dryly, "she got sick of riding the Métro."

"Was that the only reason?"

"Not quite. We'd begun to have different friends. Some of hers were pretty far out."

"Anyone in particular?"

"Crystal met an avant-garde poet — you know the type, someone who can't spell and makes a virtue of it. I couldn't stand him hanging around."

"Around your apartment, you mean?"

"Oh, he never came there. He was too pure of heart to be caught in an apartment in the Roule. It was all right for Crystal to buy his dinner and pay for his drinks, though. What a phony. He crept out of the woodwork wherever we went. Crystal and I did a lot together at that time."

"I understood that you were very close."

"Were, yes. He wasn't our kind; neither were his long-winded friends. That's what Crystal liked about him, of course. She had to be irresistible to everybody. She couldn't resist —" He broke off and shrugged. "She was just using him. He was one of the props, that's all."

"I'm not sure I understand."

"No? What did Mother tell you about us? What did she say?" His voice was still smooth, but I sensed a sudden anxiety beneath his urbane manner.

"Your mother assured me that you and your sister were extremely talented and creative," I said carefully.

Edward was not mollified. "She thinks we're wasting our time here."

"I'm not so sure. I think she just wants you to come home. That's not exactly unusual."

"We had a great time the first year we were here — until Crystal met her 'poet.' We studied the theater and how it relates to life. We experimented with controlling our lives as if we were our own characters. You might say we produced scripts for living." The beautiful indigo eyes sparkled, and as the light filtering through the chestnut trees wavered across his face, I had an intimation of some quick, living thing stirring behind his wide forehead, large eyes, and fine strong neck, something that only came out in the shadows. Edward talked on. It was soon clear that he knew a great deal about drama, and his conversation ran to technical matters of which I was ignorant. What struck me, however, was not his obvious intelligence, but rather a sense that there was something artificial about him. For a person of twenty, he was oddly lacking in spontaneity, and I wondered how far his theatrical experiments had succeeded. There was something sinister about converting life to drama, and despite his charm, he worried me. Sybil Blythe was right. I saw how unusual he was right away.

"It was very exciting," Edward said. "It was freedom, but it wouldn't have worked with a stranger."

"Perhaps your sister thought it might."

"Do you think so?" My naïveté stood condemned. "Anyway, she moved out and got a crummy apartment near the Sorbonne. She made 'another life,' as she called it."

"So you haven't seen very much of her recently?"

"Not until about a month ago."

"What happened then?"

"She'd gotten bored with him, of course, and wanted rid of him."

His phrasing was unpleasant, but perhaps it was just his intense satisfaction at being vindicated.

"We saw the possibilities for another production. I won't bore you with the details, but Crystal decided to disappear, and we staged it."

"What about her poet?"

"He decided he didn't want to be suspect number one."

"You're telling me that it looked as if Crystal had been injured?"

" 'Met with foul play' is the proper phrase, Miss Peters," he corrected smugly. "Yes, that was the general impression. The 'poet' thought it best to leave. He even cleaned out all the stuff he'd had in Crystal's room."

"I don't suppose he saw the — "

"The poetic aspects? No, he was a fake."

"I think even a Byron or a Keats would be alarmed under those circumstances, especially if she didn't turn up."

"Byron would have reveled in it, but of course you're right. From a dramatic standpoint it all went very well, but we really didn't mean to cause trouble."

He sipped his beer, and I told myself that after all he was twenty and Sybil Blythe's son.

"Then, when I didn't hear from her, I thought it was odd," he continued. "I tried to contact her in Normandy — no answer. Then I really got worried."

"Where was she staying?"

"In Caen." He reached into his pocket and pulled out a postcard. "But she's not there now, and hasn't been for nearly two weeks."

"And that letter your mother received — was that genuine?"

"Yes and no." He looked embarrassed. "I wrote it, but I was still in contact with Crystal at the time. I don't know why I did that. I should have let her pick up the pieces herself for a change."

"And then?"

"And then she stopped calling me."

"Perhaps she was just elaborating on the script. That must always be a temptation."

"She wouldn't do that to me," he replied sharply. "Something's happened to her. You must take this seriously."

"I haven't come thousands of miles to make jokes," I reminded him.

"No, of course not. I'm awfully worried, that's all."

That, at least, seemed genuine. "I understand. What do you think happened?"

"Her boyfriend left Paris at just about that time."

"Are you sure?"

"Well, he isn't hanging out at his usual places."

"That doesn't mean he went to Normandy."

"No, but it's the best explanation. I wonder if I shouldn't go to the police after all."

"We may have to, but since you've waited this long, you might as well wait a little longer and see what I can do. Your mother hinted very strongly that a police investigation, a scandal, might jeopardize your and Crystal's inheritance. That's why I'm here."

"I know, that's why I waited, but I'm not sure you can help."

"That remains to be seen."

The tables around us were beginning to fill up with Parisians ordering their aperitifs, and waiters squeezed back and forth between the tight rows of metal chairs with drinks and parfaits precariously balanced on trays held above their heads. A serious discussion was becoming impossible, but I still had two questions, and the sooner I had his answers the better. I took out a pad and pencil.

"You'd better give me the poet's name, and his address, too, if you know it."

"Crystal always called him 'Gaby,'" he said, "but he signed his work Gabriel Celestin."

I wrote this down.

"He had a room somewhere in the Latin Quarter. We always met him in a café near the Luxembourg, but I'll try to find out for you."

"You haven't tried to locate him?"

"I've asked at the café and around the Sorbonne. These types aren't often at home even if they have one. I'll take you around tomorrow, if you like, and show you Crystal's apartment and see if we can't meet some of her friends. That would help, wouldn't it?"

"Yes, it would. Tomorrow morning?"

"Afternoon. I'm tied up tonight and tomorrow morning — business, unfortunately," he answered in a breezy tone. "I'll meet you here at one, and please have dinner with me tomorrow night — your friend, too. It's the least the Blythes can do."

"Thank you, we will."

Edward was all smiles.

"There's one other thing," I said as I untangled myself from the café furniture.

"What's that?" he asked.

"Did Crystal really go to Normandy?"

"What do you mean?" he asked, surprised. "Of course she did. I just explained that to you."

"Yes, I know what you said, but your little production would have worked just as well if she'd stayed right in your apartment, wouldn't it?"

He laughed. "Economy of means? I'm afraid there are too many people around my apartment for that."

"Are there? It was just a thought. See you tomorrow."

By the time I reached the corner, he had ordered another beer and was looking pensive. An odd man. It would take a fine sieve to sort out what was genuine in him from what was fake, and yet, influenced no doubt by his spectacular good looks, I felt somewhat sorry for him. Careful about that, I scolded myself, and before I changed for dinner, I called Bertrand Gilson to ask for further information about my two dubious assistants.

*

It stayed hot and dry, and clouds of dust hung over the white paths of the Tuileries. Harry and I sat on a bench behind the Jeu de Paume and recovered from two hours of admiring Degases, Monets, and Renoirs within its poorly ventilated confines. Harry had opened a large map and was making plans for the afternoon. I was considering my appointment with Edward and wondering if Tony had found any leads.

"Where's the car Tony had the other day?" Harry asked.

"In the hotel garage. The concierge has the keys."

"Is Tony busy? I like being chauffeured around."

"I tried to call him this morning but got no answer. He's still on the job, I guess, but I'd much rather he were safely off entertaining you."

"Why's that?"

"He's going to be nothing but trouble."

"Did Gilson have a line on him?"

"He's got someone working on it, but the preliminary report isn't good· our genial tour guide spent three years in Army Intelligence, and there seems to be some difficulty in tracing his movements from then until he showed up as a translator six months ago."

"No Paris-by-Night Tours or souvenir T-shirts? What an imagination."

"They may have been real, but they were a while ago — before the Army. It's a nuisance. If he's not the idiot he seems to be, then we've got to keep him around until we can find out what his game is."

"What about our other friend, the one who's going to wine and dine us tonight?"

"Very gorgeous, very charming, and very odd. I'm curious about what you'll think of him." I gave Harry a synopsis of Edward's dramatic theories.

" 'My life's my work of art' sort of thing?"

"Sounds like it, but maybe it's gone further than usual."

"Refuge of the lazy," he remarked with the professional's contempt for the dilettante.

"Or the mediocre?"

"Isn't theirs politics, or am I scrambling the quotation?"

"It's too scrambled for me already. I'd better go, Harry. What are you going to see this afternoon?"

"The Rodin Museum, then I have appointments to show my prints to a couple of galleries."

"Good luck."

"You, too."

We separated at the Place de la Concorde, and I managed a slice of pâté, bread, and a glass of wine at the café before Edward arrived, resplendent in his white Porsche. He braked abruptly in front of my table, sending the drivers behind him to their horns, and swung open the door.

"*Bonjour,* Miss Peters." If I had aroused certain anxieties the previous day, all was forgiven.

"Are you familiar with Paris?" he asked as I climbed into the car's low-slung seat.

"Not at all."

"Pleasure before business, then. Paris is an education in itself. When I think that I might have wasted my time at home, graduating — now there, for example, that's where Talleyrand lived. He appeals to you, I imagine, and the guillotine was set up over there, right by the gates to the Tuileries. They fought all through those pretty gardens, too. Louis the Fifteenth had to nip out the back way while the people massacred his Swiss Guards. You can learn a lot from Paris," he added. "It's full of cautionary tales."

"I didn't know you were interested in history."

"This is the painless way. There was also a Tuileries Palace, that Catherine de Médicis built. It burned in the riots of the nineteenth century, and a pack of Corsicans took what was left back home to build a palace and spite the Bonapartes. That's good, don't you think?"

"It has class."

"And it's grandiose. That's the only kind of revenge, theatrical and grandiose. You'll be able to see Notre-Dame in a few minutes."

I wondered how Tony's Paris tours compared to Edward's. "What's that?" I asked, pointing to a Gothic spire rising out of a solid block of offices.

"The Sainte-Chapelle. It's surrounded now by the Palais de Justice. You should visit it — it was Saint Louis's church, and the offices are the law courts. Another revolutionary landmark. That was *the* prison during the Reign of Terror. Everyone who was anyone was there. And here, see this bridge — this is where Pierre Curie was run over by a horse van. That's what I like about Paris. All the historical sites involve sex, riots, or violent death — no dull monuments."

Edward elaborated on this theme. He seemed to be enjoying

himself, and while my more cynical side noted that he loved an audience, my better nature perceived that he was lonely. And that seemed strange: rich, young, clever, and breathtakingly handsome, Edward Blythe seemed born for social success.

"You must miss Crystal," I remarked as we turned onto the Boulevard Saint-Michel.

"Yes, but if I had the choice, I'm not sure I'd want to be twins again."

"Perhaps your sister came to the same conclusion."

"Maybe, but she always went to extremes. After she moved out, she ran with a rough crowd. She changed a great deal. I've been thinking over what you suggested yesterday — that she might be playing a joke on me. I'd never have thought that possible before."

"But you do now."

"Now I'm thinking it over," he replied cautiously. "This is it," he added, pulling up near Crystal's apartment. "To the right, the unwashed, to the left, the poetical."

We found the concierge, who greeted me without a sign of recognition, and went through the motions of inspecting Crystal's room. Normally I would have considered this play-acting a waste of time, because the sensible thing would have been to go to Caen and trace Crystal from there. But this wasn't an ordinary situation. Whether he knew where she was or not, I was gambling that Edward was the key to his sister. If he was willing to waste his time in Paris, so was I.

"Shall we go?" he asked finally.

"Yes, I think so." As I closed the closet door I noticed only one pair of riding boots. I was sure there had been two pairs the day before.

"Ready?"

"Just one other thing, the jewelry box on the bureau. Could you open it for me?"

"Open it? What for?"

"No reason. Feminine curiosity, if you like."

"Sure. As long as it isn't professional efficiency." He lifted a china cat from the floor by the fireplace and picked up the key beneath it. "Here you go. She hasn't stolen the crown jewels, you know."

Instinct pays off occasionally, and this was one such occasion. The monkey pendant was gone. As I poked at the bracelets and necklaces, it occurred to me that only one person was likely to have taken it. If Edward noticed its absence, he gave no sign. "Thank you, Edward." I handed him the key. "We can go now."

We did not visit the strange bookstore with the dirty windows and radical literature. Instead, we stopped at a bistro on the boulevard, where we learned that Gaby had been absent for nearly two weeks. Then we left the Latin Quarter for other neighborhoods. From our tour I got the impression that Crystal's life had consisted of an uninterrupted round of parties. We spoke to waiters, bistro proprietors, and nightclub managers, all of whom remembered *"la belle Crystal."* We visited swank restaurants and seamy Pigalle dives. We were unable, however, to locate anyone who might have been a friend or more than a casual acquaintance. "Everyone's away this time of year," Edward said apologetically, but I wondered if he was constructing an accurate picture of his sister. As we drove I listened to him carefully. As with his mother, the shades of feeling were more important than what was actually said. Edward seemed clever and amusing in a malicious way that one did not immediately recognize as being malicious. He was helpful and lonely and anxious, yet he was very much in the spotlight at the moment, and I couldn't help feeling that he liked it.

"Crystal has a lot of riding clothes."

"Crystal couldn't live without horses, not for anything."

"Where does she ride?"

"There are several places in Paris."

"Where does she ride most often?" I persisted.

"She boards a horse in the Bois. So do I, in fact."

"Let's go there."

"If you're sure — it's at the other end of the city," he said reluctantly.

I was sure. Forty-five minutes later, we parked in front of a massive stone stable. Riding trails led off through the trees, and there were two large riding rings, one set with hurdles, the other filled with youngsters on fat black and brown ponies. We crossed the yard, and after Edward had a short conversation with one of the grooms, we entered the cool, dim confines of the stable. Ponies and hunting hacks stuck their heads over the doors, and there was a pleasant smell of straw, horses, and polished leather.

"This is Crystal's mare," Edward said, stopping before a dapple gray with a fine head. "Careful, she nips; that one is mine." He pointed to a bay that was watching him with interest. Then the screen door at the end of the stable swung open, and a stocky, ruddy-faced man with black hair and a neat goatee appeared, carrying his tack under his arm.

"Well, hello, Edward. Are you riding today?"

"Hello, Jared. We're just checking the horses," Edward replied and turned to me. "Let's go, there's nothing else to see."

He was so obviously anxious to avoid the horseman that I was inclined to linger.

"We were admiring Crystal's horse," I said. "I don't know anything about horses, but she looks very nice."

"Yes, bit of Arab, I'd say, from the head." He took a sugar lump out of his pocket, and the mare picked it daintily from his hand. "Takes a real rider to handle her. I'm Jared Morgan," he added. "Any word from Crystal yet, Edward?"

"No, that's why I'm here," I said before Edward could reply. "Anna Peters, I'm a friend of friends."

"I think we ought to go if we're to make dinner tonight on time. Sorry to rush away, Jared."

"Have you seen Gaspare yet? He was saying something about Governor being off his feed. He's in the tack room now. Why don't you check? You know how he is."

Edward hesitated and glanced at his horse. "Gov looks all right."

"Go ahead, Edward," I said. "It's barely four; we have time."

"I'll just be a minute." Outmaneuvered, he gave Jared an angry look and stomped down the corridor.

Jared shifted his tack, waiting until Edward left the stable. "She's still missing, isn't she?"

"That's how it looks, anyway."

Jared Morgan had black eyes to match his hair and a shrewd, trustworthy face. The beard and his stoutness made him seem mature and substantial, but I guessed he was no more than a couple of years older than Edward.

"Do you know the Blythes well?"

"Well as it's possible, I'd say. They, uh, they find it hard to be friendly. That's part of the problem."

"The problem?"

"Where are you staying?" he asked in reply.

I told him.

"I'll go now," he said, as the door opened at the far end of the corridor. "Gaspare had nothing to tell Edward. I'll be in touch."

"What about?"

"I'll call you tomorrow," he replied and walked away.

"I couldn't find Gaspare anywhere," Edward said. "Jared," he called, but his friend didn't look back.

"He's like an old woman," Edward complained. "Always sticking his nose into other people's business. Governor looks fine, anyway."

I agreed that Jared had a great interest in other people's horses and said he'd told me all about Crystal's. That didn't satisfy Edward, and as we drove back to the center of the city, he was quiet and thoughtful.

"We're going right by my apartment," he said after a lengthy silence. "You won't mind stopping for a moment, will you? You can see that Crystal's not there."

"I believed you when you told me she wasn't, but I don't mind at all. I can take a cab back, for that matter."

"Oh, no, I'll drive you. I forgot to call the restaurant, that's all." He gave me one of his perfect smiles and stopped before an impressive town house. "I rent half of it," he remarked as he unlocked the front door. "It has a nice garden."

It certainly had a handsome entrance, and the apartment itself was elegantly decorated, with antique paneling on the walls and good furniture on the marble floors.

"Damn. I don't know why Mathilde can't pick up the mail instead of leaving it in a heap under the post box." He scooped up a handful of letters and bills and dumped them on a chest without looking at them. "Make yourself comfortable. I'll be right back," he said and disappeared through the living room.

I looked out at the garden and then gave in and began flipping through the mail, keeping one eye on the living room door. There was a heavy blue envelope with Sybil Blythe's name on the back, and down in the bottom of the pile, a telegram from the States, trapped in the fold of a newspaper. I was almost certain it was from his mother and stuck it hastily in my purse. The letter was further temptation, and as I heard the door opening, I succumbed and filched it, too. If Sybil Blythe was sending out bulletins on me, I felt entitled to advance notice.

# Chapter 6

**IF THERE IS A DRAWBACK** to my relationship with Harry, it is that occasionally he is too moral for comfort. To Harry, stealing Edward's mail was unethical, not sensible, and when he walked in as I was halfway through Mrs. Blythe's letter, I foresaw one of our infrequent disagreements.

"Did you have any luck?"

"None at one gallery, hope at another, and a good time at the Rodin Museum," he replied, carefully setting his portfolio on a chair. "What have you been up to?"

"I have been squired around Paris all afternoon by Edward."

"Edward the Handsome," he corrected with just a hint of distaste.

"Edward the Rich. His grandmother died last night."

"Does he know yet?"

"No, and we're not going to tell him for a while."

Harry noticed the telegram then, and picked it up. "Is this wise?" he asked.

"Necessary. His mother promised not to tell him that I was coming. She didn't keep her promise."

Harry gave me a quizzical look. "So?"

"I'm sure Crystal's back in Paris — if she ever left. I don't know if Edward's aware of that — I don't know what to think about him — but I'd like to be the one to give him the news about his grandmother."

"Why?"

"If this business with Crystal is some kind of joke, it's gone far enough. If it isn't, I'd like to know what Edward's part in it is. I want to see how he reacts to inheriting a fortune."

"Think he wants it all?"

"People have done more for less," I replied, "and he and his sister haven't been on the best of terms. One of their friends is going to call tomorrow. He said he had something to tell me, and I think it could be important." I folded the stiff blue paper that held the latest lamentation from Sybil Blythe, put it in the envelope along with the telegram, and stuck both in the back of my bag. Harry looked reproachful but said nothing, and I knew better than to court his approval. That would precipitate an argument; as it was, we were in for a cool spell. The next time I saw Bertrand Gilson, I'd tell him what I thought about his schemes.

*

Soft waves of yew and boxwood lapped the edges of the terrace, and the faint aroma of Lanvin and Guerlain mingled with the scent of oleander and geranium. Harry sat next to me, quietly devouring a mousse worth a day's wages, and across from us the candlelight flickered on Edward's blond hair and the white of his cuffs. A waiter lifted the half-empty bottle of sweet sauterne. I shook my head, but Edward had another glass. He was drinking a lot of wine — more than was good for him, and more, I suspected, than he usually did. And when he drank he was not so pleasant. Had I been alone, I probably would have broken down and had a cigarette.

He had picked us up at seven-thirty. Harry, I must say, had made every effort with him, probably because he felt guilty about the stolen mail. They talked about galleries and printmakers while I studied the menu and watched the limpid Parisian light fade into grays and golds.

"No," Harry said sharply. "I don't agree with you. That's just exhibitionism. Disgusting, too."

"What is?" I asked.

"The fellow who kills rats and things as part of his so-called artwork."

"I don't see why that isn't legitimate," Edward protested. "The aim of art is to stir emotion and to provoke thought. You're eating a trout right now — they're beautiful fish, certainly more beautiful than some old rat — and you don't care."

"The rat was burned," Harry said mildly. "It didn't die to feed the hungry."

"Look at all the barbarities practiced in the name of haute cuisine — pâté de fois gras, for instance. These people make works of art out of suffering animals and then eat them. What's the difference?"

"They don't turn their slaughterhouses into theaters, though," I said, annoyed. Suffering animals kill my appetite. "That's the difference."

"It would be more honest. Take the man who shot himself in New York as part of his exhibit. There's a pure example — no pitiful rats to worry the sentimental," Edward said with a contemptuous glance at me.

Harry drank some of his wine. "It's the same thing as far as I'm concerned," he said. "It's a way for a person without talent to gain attention. It's dishonest."

I said I thought it was rather sick. Harry nodded and began to eat his trout without pondering its aesthetic implications, but Edward continued to argue. "All the visual arts are impure," he said finally.

"Why do you say that?" I asked, curious.

"Because they depend on applause. They're made to last, to be preserved. They are not their own excuse."

"If they didn't last, if they weren't made to be sold, the poor artists would go broke. That's a rich man's argument."

"You miss," Harry said, "the great advantage of shooting yourself once in a while. You can hold down another job instead of spending all your time at an easel."

"That is incidental," Edward replied, refusing to treat the idea as a joke. "It has nothing to do with what's essential to art. Now dance and theater are different, they exist only in the moment."

"Unless they're filmed," I suggested.

"Bastard art. No, the purest art would be dance without an audience."

"Or theater without an audience?"

Edward smiled. The candlelight flickered in his eyes, and I remembered his extraordinary account of his first year in Paris.

"Nonsense," Harry said. "Theater, and all art, depends on communication."

"Carry that too far," Edward said superciliously, "and you wind up writing cheap romances and illustrating comic books."

"True enough, but to go to the other extreme just means you're afraid of competition and criticism. At some point art must become a public activity. Even the old Chinese painters had their audience, the select circle with whom they communicated."

Edward started to reply, then smiled and changed the subject, asking if we'd gotten to the cinémathèque. He and Harry discussed Henri Langois and a new Godard film that hadn't yet been released at home. I stayed out of the conversation. I felt the effort Edward was making, and it made me uneasy. I had the peculiar impression that his looks and charm were a burden he always had to live up to, as though his physical appeal were a particularly awkward parcel he was struggling to carry through a narrow doorway or up a crowded stair. There was something artificial and calculated about his manner, and there was a sensibility underneath that couldn't stand contradiction, not even in conversation.

The long formal dinner continued that way: Edward's arrogance almost, but not quite, suppressed by good manners. The more he drank, the more I thought we were likely to have a quarrel. Harry, as usual, was calm and good-natured, the worst possible antagonist for Edward.

"That was an excellent dinner," Harry said when we finished. I pushed a few soft pink raspberry fragments around my plate.

"We'll have some coffee now. Garçon! Crystal and I used to come here often, before she started screwing around with the wrong crowd," Edward confided hoarsely.

He was now quite drunk. Had I been alone with him, I would have anticipated learning something of interest. With Harry along, I had a cowardly urge to head off a scene that was sure to be unpleasant.

"I'm confident that we'll find Crystal," I said.

"Why is that?" Edward asked sharply.

"It's just a matter of time, the way things are shaping up."

"I wouldn't be too sure. Crystal's clever when she wants to be, and so am I," he added in an acid voice, "not like the hired hands."

"Let's go, Anna," Harry said abruptly.

"I'll drive you back."

"You're not only drunk, you're offensive. We'll take a cab." Harry stood up, and I could see that he was angry.

"You don't like me much, do you? I have that effect on older men. But it's not surprising."

Harry started to say something, but I pulled his arm, "Not here," I urged.

"You're leaving? Good night," Edward murmured smoothly, "and I'll have some more wine. Tomorrow, when I can appreciate it, you must tell me how you're going to find Crystal, Anna." He laughed and added, "When your protector's off duty, of course," and laughed again.

I felt embarrassed, more for Harry than for myself, and replied, "We have a lot to discuss, Edward, starting with Gabriel and those missing books."

Edward's eyes narrowed, but before he could reply the maître d' appeared. *"Bonsoir, madame, monsieur."* He ushered us out politely but quickly. This, I suspected, was a tribute to Harry's size and Edward's reputation.

"I'm sorry, Harry, I should have gone alone," I said when we were outside. "I didn't realize he drank."

"I'm glad you didn't. He's a real little prick. I can see why you stole his mail. I only wish I'd taken a swing at him."

"You touched some sore spots."

"Pretentions, you mean," Harry said, straightening his jacket with a precise, aggressive gesture.

"No, I get the feeling that he means what he says. He's probably tried to put all those crazy theories into practice."

"No wonder his sister left."

"Uh-huh, but I think he was telling the truth when he said she came back. I suppose that artistic mumbo jumbo is a way of controlling life. They seem to have had a disorganized childhood: no friends, half a dozen houses, unstable mother — the kind of life that drives some people into the Marines."

"So the Blythes indulge in creative living and pick up some artistic credit along the way?"

"Something like that. I feel a bit sorry for him."

Harry laughed. "If I looked like that, women would feel sorry for me, too. 'Poor Harry,' they'd say, 'an unappreciated artist.'" He dabbed at his eyes. "It's enough to make me cry."

I poked him in the ribs. "Be serious for a moment. What I mean is that he can't live up to his appearance."

"Who could? I can't wait to meet his sister."

"Now she's a different story altogether, from what I hear."

"I think I could learn to tolerate a beautiful heiress."

"Her brother's part of the package, remember."

"On second thought, I'll put up with you." He draped his arm across my shoulders.

"That's a romantic declaration."

"It's the city."

"It's all that food and wine."

"Materialist. No, it's in the air. The hotel's not far — shall we walk?"

"On a night like this — of course."

We walked lazily under the chestnut trees. By the time we reached our rooms, we were feeling very contented with each other. Then the phone rang.

"Damn," said Harry.

"Hello. *Allô?*"

"Anna? It's Tony. Get the car and meet me as soon as you can. The Trocadéro Gardens. They're easy to find."

I suspected Tony of contagious melodrama and said as much. His voice went up half an octave, and I realized he was scared.

"I'll explain when you come. Drive up the Avenue de New-

York. It's not far. I can't stay at the phone," he said, and the line went dead.

"I've never been to the Trocadéro Gardens," I said to Harry as casually as possible.

"I'll drive you."

"You don't need — " I began.

"They're very close. I might as well see them again. You never know when my patron may decide to cut off the cash."

\*

The gardens were dark, and the fountains in the wide trench down the middle had been turned off. Across the Seine, the Eiffel Tower spanned the night like a giant cobweb. Tony was not waiting for us. My first impulse was to head back to the hotel, lock the door, and take the phone off the hook. "I think we can park up ahead," I told Harry.

He slowed the car and steered it neatly between two dozing Citroëns. "Handles nicely." He switched off the motor and the lights. "What now?"

"Let's wait a minute."

Street lights flickered in the river like discarded diamonds, and the façade of the Palais de Chaillot was illuminated, but the slope from the formal terrace to the edge of the river was splashed with shadow. Tony did not appear.

"We'd better look for him," I said. "You take one side, I'll take the other. If we don't find him by the time we get to the top, we'll go home."

We began at the base of the ceremonial half-moon of greenery and concrete. On each side of the central plaza was a series of narrow stairs leading down from the rolling, treed lawns. Nothing moved in those shadowed alcoves; the only sounds were the scuffing of my sandals and, off to the left, the crunch of Harry's shoes on the gravel. The terrace, the statuary, the classically positioned shrubs, stood expectantly, as if a chorus was about to enter, the dancers running on stage, canes tucked stiffly under their arms. I started down one of the meandering paths: it seemed that, even with Harry, I wasn't destined to find romance in Parisian parks.

A light moved behind the trees, forcing me onto the grass to muffle my footsteps. A rustic wooden sign pointed to the aquarium. In the dimness ahead was something resembling a huge piece of volcanic rock or an immense moldy cheese. There were skylights in the roof, and when I reached the steps to the interior, I found, instead of the scent of cheese or moon dust, a damp, stony, slimy odor and a sign: ADMISSION .75 FRANCS. The entrance was blocked by a low rail and the turnstile between the ticket booths.

"Antoine? Tony?" The grotto swallowed my whisper.

There was no sound, not even the faint tap of Harry's feet on the steps. I retraced my path, pushed aside a cluster of bushes, and started up the slope toward the museum. Then footsteps exploded on the path ahead, as loud in the stillness as a troop of cavalry, and I heard a scuffle. Three figures sprang forward, and the distant lights flashed off Tony's round glasses.

"Tony!" I called, loud enough for Harry to hear.

The figures stumbled, a shoulder knocked me off balance, and I heard hoarse growls and caught the sharp smell of sweat. Tony and one of his pursuers rolled on the grass, a pinwheel of flailing arms and legs. The second man hesitated between the fight and its undesirable witness, then ran at me. I threw up an ineffectual arm, kicked him in the ankle, and landed on my hands and knees on the sandy, graveled path. I picked up a handful of grit and threw it at him, a stratagem that works in books and movies but that, believe me, is less potent than a left hook, a right cross, or a good combination. He aimed a kick at my head, and I pitched over onto the grass, felt it graze my shoulder, and saw the man turn to Tony. Someone screamed. I scrambled up. Tony lay on the ground with the two men punching and kicking him. I ran at the nearest one and hit him hard enough in the back so that he gasped and whirled, his fists swinging wildly. I ducked. His partner shouted. I heard Harry running down the path; then there were confused sounds of punches and obscenities, and I found myself hanging onto a man with a mustache and gold teeth. Tony had gotten to his feet somehow, and he swung groggily, the blow sliding off my arm. The man with the mustache lunged, breaking my grip, and fled into the darkness. A Klaxon sounded ominously in the distance.

"I've got this one," Harry said triumphantly, his arm locked around the man's neck. He held the fellow a good six inches off the ground.

"Let him go, Harry! The police are coming."

"We'll tell them what happened."

"No! We've got to get out of here."

His prisoner leaped like a fish and almost broke free. Harry snatched at his hair.

"Let him go!" I cried.

The man raced crazily down the steep path and disappeared over the edge of the wall. There were voices above us, and a second police Klaxon sounded on the bridge.

"The aquarium," Tony whispered. His face was cut, and he squinted without his glasses.

Harry grabbed Tony's arm, and between us we half-steered, half-dragged him into the shadows. A flashlight played on the trees, and we could hear footsteps coming down from the terrace.

"I don't want them to find me," Tony whined.

"Shhh," I cautioned.

I stumbled on the steep dirt slope behind the grotto, and we almost dropped Tony. Harry grabbed at a bush, and we landed, gasping and frightened, in the jagged embrace of a rangy privet.

A voice barked orders behind us. Tony found his feet and staggered forward. We scrambled around the shrubbery and onto the steps.

"Quietly," Harry whispered, and I forced myself to creep slowly down. Tony held the iron banister and edged dizzily into the grotto. At the bottom, Harry stepped lightly over the barrier, but Tony, shorter and still dizzy, swayed against the rail and nearly fell. The voices had reached the back of the grotto, and someone stumbled, as I had, on the loose dirt at the side. Harry grabbed Tony's shoulders, I lifted his legs, and we hauled him inside. Then I slid under the turnstile and into the shadows.

The stone floor was uneven, but Harry kept his arm around Tony. The grotto was lined with large aquariums set in the rock and surrounded by rough slabs and boulders that served both as seats and as steps up to the glass. Dark shapes floated in the dull fluid, and in the dim light that filtered through the skylights above the tanks, we shuffled around the back curve of the aquarium.

"Here," Tony whispered, touching my arm.

Harry helped him onto a wide, flat rock. Two, maybe three policemen stood at the barrier. A light flashed into the grotto. We ducked, and I felt the wetness on Tony's cheek and smelled the familiar scent of Harry's shaving lotion. We heard them rattling the turnstile. I looked ahead into the semidarkness of the other tunnel. There must be a door, another exit, an entrance for the attendants, I thought. Without speaking we crept farther back. My hand touched a plywood panel between the rocks but no door. Tony squeezed against it as if he intended to pass through it miraculously, while behind us a flashlight made a bright halo against a tank of long, lethal fish. We stopped breathing. The policeman followed his light, which would have swung to reveal us, crouched, undignified and disheveled, in the dank shadows if someone hadn't called excitedly from the barrier. The officer stopped and turned, his flashlight shining across a tank of moray eels. He said something, but the echoes distorted the words so that I couldn't tell if we were trapped or reprieved. Another light, and snatches of conversation. The policeman in the tunnel was wearing a raincoat, and he looked heavy and sloppy, not like one of the handsome, perfectly groomed police on duty around the presidential palace. A plain plainclothesman — and wasn't that odd for a routine disturbance call? They ran back toward the entrance, and Harry's fingers closed over my arm. Tony sank slowly down onto the floor and began wiping his face. We waited, listening to the sounds of the police outside. Then silence.

Harry said, "I'll see if they're gone."

While he moved softly down the tunnel, Tony and I stood in the pale glow of the nearest tank and tried to stop the blood that darkened the left side of his face.

"It's not deep," he said.

"Doesn't need to be." It was a nasty cut. I folded his handkerchief and one of Harry's, pressed them across his forehead, and tied them in place with my scarf.

"All clear," Harry called.

"Where's the car?"

"It's down on New-York."

"If you could bring it up the side street through the park," Tony said, "that would be safest."

Harry started for the exit.

"Better let me go instead," I interrupted. "They won't be looking for a woman, not unless they know more than is good for us. Do they, Tony?"

"I don't think so."

"Good." I crawled under the turnstile, adding another rip to my dress, and went for the car. There was a barge running on the river and a bright glow of traffic on the Avenue de New-York, but no leftover plainclothesmen. I drove slowly up the Avenue des Nations Unies. Harry and Tony were waiting at the curb, and I noticed the suit when they opened the door.

"Dammit, Tony. You were supposed to look like a French student."

"Anna! He's been badly beaten and you're complaining about his clothes. Use some sense."

"This isn't your line of work, Harry."

"I was helpful enough, though, wasn't I?"

"I'm very grateful," Tony broke in with that false, youthful eagerness I'd come to suspect. "This is some city, isn't it?"

Harry looked angry. Tony's shirt was bloody, and he was holding his side. "Are you all right, Tony?" I asked.

I could have strangled him.

"I think so."

"Do you want a doctor?"

"No, I know someone."

"Where's your apartment? Or do you want to go somewhere else?"

He didn't answer for a moment. Then, "We'd better go back to your hotel."

Harry gave him an odd look.

"Oh, it's like that," I said.

"I'll explain."

"You'd better."

He showed us where to stop along the Champs-Élysées. I went into the all-night drugstore and bought bandages and a clean shirt while Tony washed off most of the blood at one of the public fountains. We threw his filthy jacket and shirt in a trashcan and patched up his face. His eyes were swollen, but aside from that and the Band-Aids on his forehead, he looked passable.

"Let Harry have a look at your side," I said when we reached our rooms. "He knows first aid."

"I'm all right. I'll just stay here for a while."

"Then where will you go?" Harry asked, concerned. "Better wait until morning."

"Well, I — "

"Take my bed. I'll sleep with Anna."

"I think you'd better, Tony."

He didn't reply. When I went into Harry's room a few minutes later, he was lying on top of the spread. He looked sick, but he'd regained his self-possession. I sat down beside him. "Since you didn't follow my instructions, I'm assuming you were following someone else's. Care to tell me whose?"

"I've got news for you: Crystal Blythe's in Paris."

"I already knew that. I can find Crystal, thank you very much. What I'd like to know now is what you're up to."

"I work for New World Oil. I have for the past six months. You can call your home office and check it out."

"I already have, and I found out something else. Paris-by-Night Tours and Eiffel Tower T-shirts weren't your last employer, U.S. Army Intelligence was. And that suggests you're not as stupid as you've been taking pains to pretend. If you went asking questions about some radical French students in a Hathaway shirt and Hanes underwear, it was because you wanted to tip someone off. Who was that?"

"You're looking for Crystal Blythe. She's been seen in Paris. That's the information you wanted." He lay back and closed his eyes. I sighed in exasperation and left the room.

"How is he?" Harry asked.

"Stubborn and noncommunicative."

"I meant how's he feeling?"

I shrugged.

"Tony's hurt," Harry said. "I think he has bruised ribs."

"His own stupidity." I was furious, and frightened, too, because I understood how the situation could develop.

"I don't like this assignment, Anna."

"It doesn't have much to recommend it at the moment," I agreed and sat down on the bed. "Just be glad I'm not Mrs. Radford." That wasn't nice, but I wasn't feeling nice. I wasn't in the mood for moral reflections.

"That wouldn't make any difference. You don't need to be defensive."

"Offensive is more likely. Reverting to type, I'm afraid."

Harry didn't reply right away. Then, "Would you like me to go home?"

"I wish you'd never come." I leaned back on one elbow and sighed. "That's not true. I was afraid it wouldn't be a good idea, but I didn't think there'd be more involved than a messy family problem that could be solved between afternoon sightseeing and gourmet dinners."

"I know that."

"You could go to Colmar, if you'd like, or Mont-Saint-Michel. I'd like you to see some of the — "

"We should both fly home," Harry said. That was obvious, but I don't always take good advice — not even from him.

"I promised to find Crystal, and I will."

"New World will hardly thank you."

"That's not the point. And I'm not going to keep apologizing, even if I should. It's rotten work, but I'm good at it. It's like you with your prints. I get a certain satisfaction from seeing the whole design."

I checked on Tony, who was lying quietly on the bed with his eyes shut, and closed the door.

"You think I'm being hard on him, but I know what I'm doing, and I'm not at all sure he does. He nearly got himself badly hurt — and us, too. I know perfectly well what would have happened if you hadn't been there. Tony's either an innocent amateur or he's got very queer orders, but one way or another he presents a problem. He may not even be interested in Crystal, for that matter, but in her friend, Gabriel, and his friends. He lights up like a candle any time you mention Reds or radicals. That may be part of the naïve young American act or he may be some kind of fanatic, but I don't want Crystal Blythe implicated in some crazy scheme before I can get her back to the States."

"And what am I supposed to do while all this excitement's going on — ignore you and amuse myself in the galleries?"

"Something like that. It isn't your problem."

"I hate it when you're like this. There isn't a single goddamn reason for you not to trust me."

I stretched out beside him. Every relationship has its weak points: dangerous places, recurring arguments. Ours had a few of each, but Harry and I are a couple of old soldiers who know where the mines are buried. Someday maybe they'll all go off, but not yet. "How can I trust you? If you were a solid citizen, you'd be packing your bags right now. I suspect you're a dubious character after all."

"It's your influence. Mother may be right about you."

"Mother *is* right about me. I've told you all along, I'm bad company."

"No, that's the trouble. You're good company but a bad influence."

That's me, all right. But it's unfair. The things I do well always leave me feeling I've behaved badly — when really I've done the only thing possible.

# Chapter 7

THE HAY WAGON, pulled by two rough-coated plow-horses, raced over a narrow, washed-out roadbed. It was followed by a fuzzy russet mongrel who, between attempts to sever my toes, carried on an intelligent conversation. Something was loose on the wagon, something that banged and rattled until I shut out the horses hoofs and the talking dog, concentrated on the noise, and woke up. It was the middle of the night in Paris. Harry was lying asleep beside me, but there was a light on in the adjoining room, and the banging turned into the soft, surreptitious sounds of someone moving around.

I got up, pulled a pair of slacks over my nightgown, and stuck my feet into a pair of sneakers. The outer door of Tony's room opened. I grabbed my raincoat, waited until the elevator door closed, then hurried into the hall and down the main stairs. The light of the slow-moving car dropped smoothly and steadily past the grillwork on each floor. I stopped at the landing above the lobby and crouched behind the newel post as the elevator creaked to a halt. Tony stepped out, the bruises on his face a sickly greenish blue in the harsh light, and I squeezed back against the stairs. He crossed the lobby without looking up, ignored the dozing night clerk, and went out. I ran down the steps, and the fat, bald man at the desk shifted in his chair. I waited for a few seconds behind the door, watched Tony walk swiftly into the darkness, then followed him.

The night air was cool, and the deserted sidewalks were slick with moisture. As I dodged from one patch of shadow to another, I could only hope that he wouldn't turn around. I expected to be discovered each time I passed a street light or a café window, but Tony moved resolutely toward the avenue. Once, crossing a side street, he stopped to look back. I froze, only half-hidden by a garage door, but he gave no sign of recognition. Then I remembered that he'd lost his glasses in the fight. I felt better and followed him more boldly along a narrow alley and into the dense shade of a strip of parkland. Figures dozed on the benches under the inky hands of the chestnut trees, and I tied my raincoat tightly over my nightgown and walked faster. Tony crossed against the traffic and hurried into a brightly lit café — looking for a phone, probably. It was two A.M. I sat on a park bench and waited. Someone coughed nearby, and glancing across the circle of gravel, I saw light reflecting off a bottle and heard someone drinking. From the heavy foliage beside my bench came the unmistakable sounds of someone relieving himself. I walked as nonchalantly as I could to the sidewalk and positioned myself behind a kiosk. Torn posters announced a concert and a ballet and touted the Folies-Bergère and a play at the Comédie-Française. I found it difficult to read casually at that hour of the morning, and I wished Tony would hurry up with whatever he was doing. My mind raced: dammit, suppose there's a back entrance; perhaps he's seen me after all. I had started around the kiosk when a dark blue Mustang pulled up across from me. It was just like Tony to be picked up in a Ford. A man got out of the car and walked into the café. Had to be, I decided. Footsteps rustled on the grass, and I glanced back in irritation. Just some of the derelicts on the benches. I saw Tony silhouetted against the yellow rectangle of the café, and as I strained to get a better look, someone moved behind me. I didn't react fast enough. An arm snapped around my throat, and something hard pressed against my ribs.

"That's a thirty-eight," a nasal American voice said. I was in trouble.

"We're going to walk across the street," the man said, "and get into that car." Tony and the driver were already waiting there. The Mustang started.

"It would be a bitch to have to shoot you," the voice at my ear warned, "but we'd get away with it."

We crossed the street; the rear door of the car swung open, and as the gun dropped I considered calling his bluff and making a break for it but found that I lacked the nerve. I rationalized this piece of cowardice by my desire to learn who was employing Tony. As for my former translator, he sat pale, weak-eyed, and surprised in the corner. So he hadn't seen me, and the fat man on the hotel desk hadn't been sleeping, after all. Someone was going to a great deal of trouble on my account.

The springs creaked as the man with the gun got in. He was tall and on the thin side with a long, sallow face and stringy black hair. He pocketed the .38 and gave me a genial nod. The driver turned to us. "All set?" he asked. This one was a handsome, square-faced specimen in a linen jacket. He had blue eyes, a fine jaw, and the crisp Eastern Establishment diction that goes with independent wealth — an ensemble better fitted to a tailgate at the Yale-Harvard game than the wheel of a getaway car. He had nice manners, too.

"Good evening, Miss Peters," he said.

"It's morning," I responded. I wasn't feeling congenial.

"Evenings are long in Paris. Have you been enjoying your stay?"

"Up to now or including the present?"

"Don't be upset, Miss Peters. We would have found a more conventional means of contacting you, but under the circumstances — "

"I don't know what you mean by conventional. Taking the victim for a ride is traditional in some circles."

The man at the wheel laughed, but Tony spoke up nervously. "Don't push the Major, Anna. He's serious."

"I don't know about that," I said. "We haven't even been introduced yet."

"Oh, Major Smith will do for now, if you don't mind," our driver said. "Miss Peters has every right to feel alarmed, Tony. But you're among friends, I can assure you."

I've felt safer among enemies, but I didn't comment, and the conversation died. I had lost my sense of direction, although I could tell that we were heading out of the city. At last we pulled onto a track through a wide meadow, lighted by the fat lemon slice of moon. The Major switched off the motor and opened his door. "What a pleasant night. We can talk safely here, Miss Peters. Out, if you please."

The bearer of the .38 let me out, then got back into the car with Tony. Major Smith and I walked down to the river, where he lit a cigar and meditated for a moment upon the still black water.

"You don't seem particularly surprised."

"It wasn't totally unexpected."

"Why not?"

I shrugged. "That's not material, is it?" There was no point in telling the Major any more than I had to.

"It might be. It is important that you cooperate with us."

"Who's us and what about?"

"The latter first. You are looking for Crystal Blythe."

"I'm on vacation, but I'm making a few inquiries about her as a favor to her mother."

"More of a favor to New World Oil, I'd say."

"The company is interested, of course."

"I will simplify your task: Crystal is back in Paris."

"If she ever left."

He clucked gently and flipped the stub of the cigar into the river. It landed in the water with a soft fizz. "That's neither here nor there," he said, "and I'd advise you not to look into the matter further."

"No?"

"No. From now on, you and your friend, Radford, will simply be tourists. Go to all the galleries, shows, whatever you want — preferably standard tourist attractions where you'll be noticed — but no more amateur detective work. Is that clear?"

"I need a little more information first. You haven't told me who you are, and you haven't explained your interest in Crystal Blythe — or is it Gabriel Celestin you're concerned about?"

"It's a matter of national security," he said.

"A wild-eyed French poet?"

"He was that — until lately."

"And lately?"

"He's started moving in very radical company. That's why we're interested. His connection with an American oil heiress is suggestive, don't you think?"

"What about her brother?"

The Major's blue eyes flickered. "What about him?"

"He has a real dislike for Gabriel, and he's a born actor. If you're getting your information from him I'd be careful of it, that's all."

"I don't think you need concern yourself with our sources."

"Suit yourself. I hope they're better than your operatives."

"I will tell you what I want," the Major said in a crisp, commanding voice, "and you will see that I get it. Otherwise you and your artist friend will be declared persona non grata here and be shipped home. Your company wouldn't like that."

"Probably not."

"You're welcome to take Crystal home. I'll personally see that the way's clear, period, no matter what. But if you screw this up, I'll see that she stays in France, has a bad time, and blames you for it. How will that go down with the home office?"

"Not well." There are worse things than official displeasure, but I didn't mention that to Major Smith. He'd be happier if he thought that I was quivering in my shoes, and I wanted him to be happy. He took out another cigar, cut off the top, and began filling the air with its stale fumes.

"What happens if she doesn't turn up? My company won't exactly be overjoyed."

"I feel sure that the Blythe girl will turn up with or without your efforts. I don't think you need worry."

"I'm sorry, Major, but I can't take your word for that."

There was a sudden flash of light. I felt the heat on my face and flinched. The hot red eye of the Major's cigar stopped half an inch from my lashes.

"Next time, Miss Peters," he said, and he wasn't smiling. "Now please remember to do exactly as I've told you, so no one gets hurt."

I blinked, sending up flaming green coronas that ballooned

before my retina and burst in the silver night. I felt sick. We returned single file to the car. The gunman stepped out with polite caution and stood holding the door. I wanted to kick him in the shins or spit in his face. I hate being bullied. I had enough of that ten years ago when I was married and more than enough in the hard years since. But of all the kinds of bullying and thuggery, the worst is the hypocritical, incompetent, bureaucratic kind, like this, the official kind. I got in beside Tony and whispered, "I'd be sick, too, if I were you."

He turned pale. The Major slammed his door and started the motor. None of us spoke. I spent the journey back to Paris hoping I wouldn't get carsick. It's bad nerves, I suppose, but fear produces that juvenile ailment in me. The car smelled of the Major's cigar. It would be a pleasure to mess up whatever he had running at the moment.

They stopped a block from the hotel. "Less conspicuous, you understand, Miss Peters," which was a joke if they were paying the desk clerk.

On the sidewalk I glared at the Mustang and its occupants.

"We are clear, aren't we?" the Major asked.

"Harry and I will be at the Louvre tomorrow," I replied.

"Good. Enjoy Paris. I'll be in touch."

"Suppose I need to contact you?"

"My card. *Bonsoir,*" he said suavely and pulled away from the curb.

Major Smith, according to his card, was employed by Uni-World Transport Company, Inc. So that's what the local CIA was calling itself at the moment — if he really was CIA and not some other, even more dubious outfit. I memorized the telephone number, then tore up the card and dropped the pieces in the gutter. The Major looked like a serious complication, and by the time I reached our rooms, the disagreeable possibilities had multiplied like so many vermin. I opened the long windows and looked out over the chimney pots. Harry had no idea what he'd talked himself into.

\*

"Anna, it's for you. Some guy named Jared Morgan."

I sat up in bed. Harry had been trying to rouse me for some time, but that name did the trick.

"I'll call him in twenty minutes. Get his number."

"You're awake now, you — "

I shook my head. "I'll explain. Just tell him."

He did and hung up. "You're looking radiant as the dawn this morning. Aurora's a little late, though."

He didn't need to tell me. The bags under my eyes had become suitcases, and when I ran a despairing hand through my hair, I smelled the Major's cigar smoke. I turned Harry's wrist over and checked his watch — ten A.M. I groaned. There was nothing for it; I had to get up.

"Want me to order up coffee?"

"Please." I threw on my clothes and slopped cold water over the corpse. It stirred.

"I'll be right back, Harry."

"I've bought the papers already," he replied.

"Phone call — and I don't trust the desk clerk," I said and slipped out. Two minutes down to the phone booth at the tabac on the corner. Five minutes to struggle with the phone and Jared Morgan. Two minutes back. Not really long enough to figure out something neat, clever, and plausible to tell Harry. So I told him the truth. I always do. The fruit of my somewhat shady career: it's not possible to lie to everyone.

Just the same, I put the best face on it that I possibly could and concluded with the Pollyannaish idea that the latest complication might simplify everything. "If the creep I met last night gets to her, my guess is that Crystal will scurry home to Mama with Edward in tow."

"The bastard," Harry said. I wasn't sure whether he was referring to Edward or the Major, and I didn't ask.

"I told Jared I'd meet him by the Delacroix paintings at the Louvre. I might have lunch with him, too, but you don't have to bother."

"Good. I have appointments at galleries this afternoon. That will square with Major Smith's orders, won't it?"

"Ideal." He smiled, but I felt glum. I will never do a favor for Bertrand Gilson again.

The Louvre was mobbed. If you lingered too long in front of a painting, you were apt to find yourself surrounded and sucked into the amoebic, many-headed creature that formed itself from the warm, perspiring bodies of eager art lovers. If, on the other hand, you loitered in the halls or on the steps, you were sure to be run over by the neat, fast-moving battalions of Japanese, who seemed to tour only in compact, noisy groups festooned with cameras and clothed by Dior. We easily lost the man following us. He was swept clean away under the Nike of Samothrace, a perilous spot, where Harry and I had prudently separated.

Upstairs, I found a banquette set before the *Massacre at Chios* and sat down to admire the brushwork. All that voluptuous agony isn't really to my taste, but thanks to Harry, I know quite a bit about painting. I was busy imagining Major Smith's smooth, courtly visage in place of the menacing Turk's when the leather cushion next to me squealed in alarm. Jared Morgan wiped his forehead and said, "It hasn't been this hot here since the fourteenth century."

"I didn't realize."

"Yes, they're making quite a fuss over it." He opened his paper. "See: 'Hottest Ever,' 'Visit the Catacombs to Beat the Heat,' 'Record Temperatures from around Europe,' 'Climatic Changes Suspected.' They should visit Chicago in July."

"You seem to be feeling it just the same."

"This certainly is a steam bath. Shall we go outside or is there some mysterious reason why we're here?"

"Outside. Harry wanted to show me some paintings, that's all, I hope you didn't mind."

"Not at all. I'm glad you didn't invite me to your hotel."

"Why is that?"

"I'd rather not have Edward know I contacted you," Jared said as we walked down the wide steps. "I got the feeling yesterday that he'd rather not have seen me."

"I got that feeling, too. He's temperamental, though, isn't he?"

"Are you guessing or speaking from experience?"

"Experience."

"I'm an old friend of Crystal's and Edward's, Miss Peters, and I'm not fond of telling tales." He stopped on the gravel walk, a stout, earnest, red-faced man. I liked him. "We used to have a house in Connecticut near them," he continued. "Edward and I have played polo together, and I've always admired Crystal."

"That seems to be the general reaction to her," I remarked, then wished I hadn't, because his face fell, as though he remembered something painful.

"Yes," he agreed soberly, "and I might as well tell you that I was pretty far down the line. Still, I think you ought to know something about her and Edward."

"Please — if you think it would help locate her. It won't go any further."

He turned down the walk toward the Tuileries. "We had dinner together not so long ago — a month, maybe. It was sort of a reunion. We'd lost touch over the past year, although we used to do a lot together when they first arrived, and I still rode with Crystal fairly often."

"Did you see her at the stables until she disappeared?"

He gave me a curious look. "Oh, yes."

"And since?"

He looked uncomfortable. "Let me tell you what I want you to know first. It will explain a lot. As I said, we met for drinks and dinner and had a good time. Sometimes, you know, when you meet people you used to be close to and aren't anymore, it can be awkward. There wasn't any of that. It was fun. They can be so charming."

"And then?"

"We drove out to the Bois, and when we passed the stables, Crystal insisted we stop. She wanted to go riding — this was maybe eleven at night — and I said no, it was impossible. I mean, the stable hands had gone or were asleep, but Crystal and Edward were never considerate. She said Gaspare would be around, and he was, but I could see that he didn't like it. He takes good care of his horses, and we were all high, especially Edward."

Jared paused for a few minutes. "It was a beautiful night. Full moon, warm, flowers in the air — perfect. Crystal talked Gaspare into letting her ride, and she put a bridle on Queen Mab — that's the gray you saw yesterday — but no saddle, to spare the tack, you see. Edward and I watched. Crystal took her into the riding ring and set her at the fences." He shook his head. "She was in evening dress, of course. What a rider! Even Gaspare was laughing, and the upshot was that Edward and I bridled our horses, too, and we all rode off on one of the trails. Crystal was in high spirits, as she always is when she's gotten her way. She wasn't wild or showing off, she was delightful." He paused again. "I know what you're thinking. It's true, but I was enjoying myself. Crystal and I were joking about nothing, and then we passed a big bench. I think it was a bench, marble or concrete, white, anyway, and high." He lifted his hand almost to shoulder level. "I hadn't been paying much attention to Edward; when he drinks he isn't much fun. All of a sudden he dared Crystal to jump the bench and tried to persuade her to attempt it — crazy! I'm an excellent rider, and I'd have hesitated even in daylight with a saddle and the best horse in the stable. I thought for a minute Crystal would take him up on it, but vain or not, she's no fool. She just laughed at him and said that Queen Mab's legs were too valuable. Edward fell into that arrogant mood of his and insisted he'd do it. I tried to warn him, but he wouldn't listen. He rode Governor out in a wide circle. Crystal never said a thing."

"What happened?"

"Governor refused. He took one look at that hunk of stone, put his head down, dug in his feet, and Edward wound up hanging on to his ears."

I couldn't help laughing.

"It seemed funny," Jared agreed, "but it wasn't. Edward got furious. He and Crystal began screaming at one another. It was the ugliest fight I've ever seen."

"What was the reason for it?"

"He accused her of making a fool of him. No, I don't know. She's a better rider than he, but not by much. It wasn't rational. He seemed wildly jealous of her, of some guy she was seeing." Jared shrugged. "I gathered that this argument between them had been running for a while. I finally calmed them down enough to ride back to the stable. Fortunately we had my car, and I was driving. I took Edward home first and then drove over to the Latin Quarter with Crystal."

"And then?"

Jared looked very serious. "You can take my word for it — Crystal is usually fearless, even reckless. But Edward had no sooner gotten out of the car than she began to cry, really cry."

"What was wrong?"

"She told me that she was afraid of her brother."

"Because of the fight, you mean?"

"Because she thought he might try to kill her, Miss Peters."

# Chapter 8

After my talk with Jared, I walked gloomily back to the museum and sat down on the steps. Ahead, the grass and paths of the gardens burned green and white, and Maillol's plump bronzes cavorted in the brilliant sun, but beneath the massive façade the palace stairs were cool. Although I was willing to vouch for his honesty, Jared's story bothered me. I reflected on it and came to the same conclusion: there was a big piece missing. If Crystal feared her brother — which, true or not, Jared certainly believed — would she have risked an escapade with him during which her convenient "disappearance" might have been made permanent? Not likely. Suppose she were afraid of someone else — Celestin, Smith, parties unknown — or suppose she had wished to confuse Jared about Edward? About someone else? My train of thought wilted in the heat and in the knowledge that my sources had dwindled. I'd lost Tony's services, such as they were, and I doubted that I could hire another translator without alerting the Major. I couldn't trust Edward's information, and Jared, I was sure, had already told me all he knew. That left the people at the stable. I believed that Crystal still visited there, and I was wondering whether I spoke enough French to question the grooms when I spotted our tail from the morning. Yes, that was he: a skinny, washed-out blond chap with a stubble of beard and a discouraged, hangdog expression — the product, no doubt, of losing us before eleven A.M. Major Smith wouldn't be amused. The man didn't seem to have noticed me yet; he was leaning against a pillar, greedily smoking a cigarette. I felt a superior glow — I no longer wanted one — and wondered how long it had taken him to escape from the Nipponese flying wedge. The trip to the stable would have to be postponed until I lost him; for while it would have been quick and easy to leave before he saw me, if he reported that I'd disappeared at eleven from the Louvre Major Smith would think the worst. Better to let my shadow believe I'd simply been stretching my legs in the greenery all this time and lose him later in some less suspicious manner. Far better. I sauntered past him into a wide dusty room full of marble portrait heads, mosaics, heroic nudes, and cracked pots. I proceeded to make a complete circuit of oriental antiquities while my follower feigned an increasingly desperate interest in Etruscan ceramics, small Roman bronzes, and Egyptian jewelry. I consulted my watch several times during our promenade and looked around impatiently. Finally, clearly annoyed that my friend was late, I left the Louvre at the Rue de Rivoli and headed briskly toward the Métro. Satisfied by this pantomime, the man followed.

Then I found myself temporarily out of ideas: it's hard to lose a professional without tipping him off, and even assuming that Major Smith would underestimate my capacity for deception, I had to be careful. As I walked along the stifling street, my first thought was to return to the hotel and leave again by the back door or the fire escape, an unoriginal design that would fool nobody. I didn't come up with anything better until we were in the tunnel leading to the trains.

The Métro has a system of automatic doors set a couple of feet above the floor, like the swinging doors in Wild West saloons, and made of heavy steel. When a train pulls into the station, these doors close the access tunnels to prevent a last-minute dash to the cars. The warning bell started ringing as I approached the head of the tunnel and I sprinted through, but instead of joining the crowd hurrying to board the cars, I turned to the left and stepped over piles of bricks and bags of cement to the shelter of the canvas screening a wall section under repair. A dusty-faced man on a ladder looked down in surprise. Afraid that he would shout at me and alert my pursuer, I stared at the tracks as though it were the most natural thing in the world for a tourist in a yellow shirt and a pair of white slacks to wait for her train in a pile of cement dust. The engine roared in; the swinging doors had closed, and glancing around the edge of the canvas, I saw the blond man crawl under the barrier. He dashed down the platform, looking into the cars. Above me, the workman shifted on his scaffolding and yelled something that echoed through the tunnel. Here it comes, I thought, and waited for the tail to catch me red-faced and red-handed.

*"Un moment, un moment,"* someone called crossly over the noise of the train. Another workman appeared, carrying a paint can, and almost bumped into me.

*"Pardon,"* I muttered, retreating farther into the canvas alcove.

He gestured for me to come out, "crazy tourist" written all over his face.

*"Pardon,"* I repeated and politely motioned for him to pass. Wouldn't that train ever leave?

He responded in a guttural dialect, "Lady, get the hell out of there" probably, and I smiled and nodded inanely as the welcome buzzer signaled the departure of the train and the opening of the safety gate. Had he gotten off? I peered over the workman's shoulder. No. A new flood of passengers issued onto the platform. I stepped around the glaring worker to join the throng. The two workers exchanged expressions of resignation and exasperation, and I took the next train as far as the Champs-Élysées stop.

I'd decided to pick up my map before I went to visit the stable, and I had almost reached the hotel when I noticed a man leaning against one of the neighboring buildings and staring at me with undisguised interest. Another of Major Smith's minions, I figured. This one was small, weatherbeaten, and wiry, and his dirty brown sweater and tattered work pants contrasted with the polished shoes showing beneath them. He let me pass, then called softly, "Mademoiselle Peters?"

I stopped without looking back. "Yes?"

"My name is Gaspare," he said in clear, though accented, English. "Edward and Crystal Blythe know me."

I looked down at his polished shoes and saw then that they were riding boots.

"You're from the stable."

"*Bon.* Come with me, please."

"Where to?"

"You will see." We circled the block, crossed the avenue again, and walked for several minutes. Then he directed me to a wide cobblestone alleyway. A little restaurant, a boulangerie, and a patisserie shared the court with several small apartments. Parked along the street were some cars and a delivery truck and, in the driveway beside the restaurant, a green horse van. Gaspare glanced about cautiously, then tapped on the rear door.

*"C'est moi,"* he said.

The door swung open. He motioned me in. At first I thought Edward was inside, but the blonde hair was too long, and the face, despite the remarkable similarity of the features, was softer and fuller.

*"Merci,* Gaspare," Crystal Blythe said, and the door in the van closed, leaving us in a twilight dimness. The engine started. Crystal banged on the back of the cab, and the van backed out with a lurch, throwing me against the side. I grabbed at the roof to steady myself.

"Sit down or you'll get hurt," Crystal said and pulled me toward a bale of straw. She leaned against the side of the van. "Are you here to find me?"

"Yes."

"Mission accomplished. Congratulations."

"Not quite. You're needed at home."

She moved, but I couldn't read the gesture in the dimness.

"Where have you been hiding?"

"My secret."

"Your mother has been worried about you."

"Mother has undoubtedly enjoyed every minute of my absence. 'Poor Crystal — such a charming girl, so amusing. I'm sure nothing's happened to her, you understand, but — ' " She sighed exactly like Sybil Blythe and stretched her legs with a lazy, graceful gesture. "Mother, you must understand, has her own ideas of enjoyment."

"What about you?"

"Mine are more conventional."

"Then this isn't part of some amateur theatrical?"

"No, that's Edward's department," she replied tartly.

More she didn't volunteer. Unlike most people their age, the Blythes had no taste for talking about themselves, and they felt no need to fill up awkward silences. Neither do I. My eyes had adjusted to the dim light, and I took a good look at her. She was, indeed, extraordinarily like her brother, as close in appearance as the difference in sex would allow, and she had, I noticed, many of the same mannerisms, the same graceful, relaxed air of the natural athlete, the same quick smile. And as Edward's unusual beauty gave him a delicacy and subtlety unexpected in a man, so the clarity and strength of his sister's features gave her an air of activity and vigor. Despite her luxuriant hair and classic figure, there was something boyish about her that added complexity to her other attractions. So obvious were the similarities between the Blythes that I looked naturally for their differences. This was an inclination I was later to regret.

"Are you planning to go back to the States?"

"I don't think that's possible."

"I can't say that traveling by horse van is my idea of the good life in Europe. You wouldn't have to resort to this at home."

She didn't reply.

"You must have contacted me for a reason. You've gone to a modest amount of trouble. Are you going to tell me why?"

"I want to talk to you. You might be able to help me."

"If it's anything money can buy, you don't need to worry."

"What do you mean? Has Grandmother — "

"She died two days ago. You and Edward are her joint heirs."

"Oh."

I was surprised at the expression of shock on her face.

"Were you very fond of your grandmother?"

"Grandmother Blythe? She was a terror, a real old horror. Edward must — Does he know?"

"I'm not sure. It depends on how often your mother writes to him." I handed her the telegram and the letter.

Crystal rose and held them close to the window, her feet braced against the sway of the van.

"I'd like them back," I said when she finished reading.

"They don't belong to you."

"Nor to you, either. I'd better keep them, unless you want to return them to Edward yourself."

"I don't care to see Edward," she said. "Most of this is his fault."

I returned the mail to my bag. "You're going to have to confront him sooner or later. The two of you will have a lot of decisions to make when you inherit your grandmother's fortune. Many responsibilities go with it. My advice is to pack up and fly home immediately. I'm sure Edward will follow as soon as he knows. Whatever difficulties you've been having can get straightened out in the States, and if that's not possible, let your lawyers do the talking."

"I'm being watched," she said.

"By whom?"

"I know it sounds crazy." She studied the floor. "I'd better explain everything from the beginning." She looked up and fiddled automatically with the voltage of those astonishing Blythe eyes.

"Good idea."

The voltage dropped. She could have turned that fat, cigar-smoking gumshoe into steak tartare in an instant. If she got herself safely back to the States, those eyes would decimate the New World Board of Directors, and Edward would polish off the tokens and the wives: a formidable combination.

"You know that Edward and I moved to Paris two years ago?"

"Yes."

"Everything went well until I decided we needed to meet people, make friends, get out more. We started hanging out with a group of students at the Sorbonne. I mean, what's the point of living in Paris and not getting to know people? It wasn't any big deal, but Edward picked fights with some of the guys. And then we quarreled about Gaby, a friend of mine, and things got so bad that I moved out of our apartment and rented one near the university."

"Gaby — Gabriel Celestin?"

"Yes, that's how he signs his poems, anyway. His poetry is not brilliant, but he seems talented, and he's been published."

I nodded, and she resumed.

"Gaby is interested in politics, but neither Edward nor I know much about French parties or student groups. We really aren't interested. Gaby is all wrapped up in this movement and that political clique. We didn't take it seriously. It seems so melodramatic — the forces of evil materialism and capitalism, the pure virtue of improved Maoism, or whatever it is he believes in, the death struggle of this ism or that ism. We thought, well, we thought he was like us."

I remembered what Edward had told me. "In what way?"

"Edward and I are interested in the theater, in how one can create scenes within the context of daily life, how we can manipulate our emotions."

"Or other people's?"

She detected the note of disapproval and frowned. "Anyway, I got interested in Gaby and his friends, although Edward couldn't stand them. Edward's jealous, and he likes to be the star. Gaby's a natural leader."

"But you didn't think they were for real?"

"Not completely, not until later."

"And how did Gaby rationalize the fact that he was fraternizing with a pair of potential oil magnates?"

Crystal smiled slyly. "We never told him. Edward and I were just ordinary students, and then, Gaby didn't take us seriously, either. I told him I was squandering the profits of a machine tool firm. You know, busily making it decadent so the working class could take over. We all believe," she added coolly, "what suits us at the moment."

"What convinced you Gaby wasn't just playing at being a student revolutionary?"

"He began to go on trips occasionally, then more frequently. I don't know why or where, except that he went to Strasbourg a couple of times. And he dropped some of his old friends. He lost the apartment he shared that way, and he asked me to keep his political books for him."

"Did he introduce you to anyone new?"

"No, he became secretive, and he seemed excited, confident, absorbed in some plan or other. He talked about action, an end to theorizing, a chance to do something at last. By this time I was sorry I'd gotten involved with him. He was always intense. I liked that, and he was sincere, but his politics made me nervous. It would have been hypocritical of me to stay involved, and, to tell you the truth, his rhetoric began to bore me. And I missed Edward." Then, almost as an afterthought: "And the other thing that bothered me was those kidnappings in America. I knew Grandmother was sick. If we inherited her money, it would eventually get into the papers. I trusted Gaby, but not his friends, and in any case he'd realize I hadn't been honest with him."

"You got yourself in a bad spot. Why didn't you just break up with him and return home?"

"I wanted to. We wouldn't have had to live with Mother. We'll be of age soon and can do whatever we please. I was ready to go home, but Edward wouldn't leave. Or not that simply. He wanted me to disappear. I should have known better, but it was what Edward wanted, and his plan sounded like fun," she added with a negligent shrug.

"And when it got out of hand, Edward called it off."

"That's what I expected. I hadn't taken into account the changes in him."

"What do you mean?"

"My brother almost turned a simple prank into a police case implicating Gaby and his friends. He got carried away by his own creation and nearly got Gaby arrested. I panicked because they had been watching Gaby even before I left."

"Who?"

"A couple of men. He said they were government spies, but

he was always saying things like that. It was popular in his circle. Later I began to think it was true."

"What is Gaby into? Drugs, guns, plastique? He must have told you something."

"No, nothing at all. At first I didn't believe there was anything, and later I didn't want to know."

I wasn't convinced. "Why didn't you stay in touch with Edward? Or has he been lying to me?"

"Lying to you?"

"Edward claims he is anxious about you, that he hasn't heard from you in weeks."

"He hasn't. Do you think he's worried?"

"He appears to be."

"I don't understand Edward anymore," she replied with real emotion. "I don't want to see him or have anything to do with him, not here. I was hoping we'd be close again once Gaby and I split up. That's why I agreed to this crazy drama. It was for *him*. But Edward got me into trouble, and I think it was deliberate. He's unbelievably jealous."

"Has this hide-and-seek been to frighten Edward? To pay him back? Didn't you consider anyone else, your mother — "

"He almost led the police to Gaby," she interrupted angrily, "and he didn't give a damn about me."

"If you don't stop this nonsense and go home and get your name in the newspapers like a good little heiress, you're going to be talking to the police no matter what Edward does, and they're bound to ask about Gaby. They've got more important things to do than to mediate childish quarrels."

"I thought you were here to help," she snapped.

"Right, and the best way to do that is to put you on an airplane for home tomorrow. I'll go straight to the airlines and make the arrangements. If you insist on avoiding Edward, let me know where to pick you up and it will all be done discreetly." Discretion was beginning to leave a sour taste.

"But suppose Edward — "

"Suppose Edward what? What are you afraid of?"

"Nothing, but Edward's been up to something."

"Listen, forget Edward — and Gaby, too. It'll be best for both of them. Once you're in the States, Edward will have no choice but to come home or hire lawyers to handle his share. And if your conscience bothers you about Gaby, send him a fat check to finance the revolution."

Crystal chewed on her lower lip, looking cross. She was used to being handled with kid gloves, and she didn't like being scolded. I'd have enjoyed walloping both the Blythes.

"You'll make the arrangements?"

"Yes, don't worry, and if you don't want to see Edward you don't have to. That's a promise."

"You can reach me through Gaspare."

"At the stable?"

"Yes, he lives there."

"All right, that's set then." If it was all set, why did I feel so uneasy? The van was jouncing uncomfortably. "Where are we?"

"We're there now — at the stable. I'll get out here, and Gaspare will take you back."

The van pulled to a halt. Gaspare opened the door of the cab to an unwelcome sound.

"Gaspare," Edward called, "bring the van around, would you? There's a horse here to go out."

Crystal swore. "He mustn't know I'm here."

"One moment. I'll drive it to the back," he added, closer to the door. "Not here, it will scare the children's classes. I have stuff to empty out."

"Well, hurry it up, Gaspare."

The engine started again, and the van bumped over a rough track around the back of the stable and stopped, the motor humming. Gaspare wrenched open the door to the van.

"Get out quickly. I'll explain later."

Crystal jumped nimbly down and I followed. The back of the stable was surrounded by large trees, and the yard wore a comfortable, tumbledown, overgrown air. Behind us, at the edge of the clearing, was a large pile of old straw and manure. The building itself showed a solid wall of heavy stones, broken only by a small door and, high above, a loading entrance to the loft.

"In here," Crystal said. We ran for the door and the dim, horse-smelling corridor. A groom whistled, and a tethered horse stamped restlessly on the stone floor.

"Gaspare, where the hell's that damn van?"

"Come on, you can leave through the front," Crystal said, and she led the way past the rows of stalls. Ahead, the main entrance glowed in the sunlight. A child passed, leading a spotted pony, and then a man stepped into the chartreuse square of lawn and lighted a cigar. I grabbed Crystal's arm. "Don't go out there."

"Why not?" She looked behind us anxiously.

"He's one of the people after Gaby," I said.

She had quick reactions and didn't ask useless questions.

"Back this way."

"I'll get it, I'll get it," Edward yelled from the rear, and the door behind us opened. Instinctively Crystal headed toward where the Major stood, his cloud of blue smoke mingling with the scents of horses and roses. I pulled her behind the shelter of a half-open stall door.

"He's coming in here."

She jerked away and motioned for me to follow her. A ladder hung on the wall at one end of the corridor, and she scrambled up, knocked open a trap door, and climbed into the loft. I was sure the Major would notice, but he continued to puff his cigar.

"Hurry," Crystal commanded.

My sandals slipped on the smooth rungs, but she leaned down and helped me up; then we replaced the door. Crystal sat on a bale of straw, and I walked the length of the huge loft and peered out the tiny windows under the eaves. The Major's blue Mustang was parked in front, as was Edward's white Porsche. I began having second thoughts about Edward.

"Why is that man here?"

"I don't know. Do you have any ideas?"

"Is Edward talking to him?"

"I can't hear anything."

She knelt at the center of the loft. We heard a faint murmur below, and Crystal opened one of the hay chutes.

"Take care," Edward said.

"You, too, and my congratulations, Edward," the Major replied.

Boots clicked down the corridor, and a door banged in the rear of the stable. We headed for the ladder. Someone was whistling almost directly beneath us.

I bent to lift the hatch door, but Crystal stopped me. "We can't. I don't want to see Edward."

"Is there another way out?"

The whistling increased in volume as someone climbed the ladder.

"We'll drop down into one of the stalls."

I didn't fancy that, but Crystal couldn't be dissuaded. "This chute is empty."

"Where's the Major?"

"I can't see him, but we've got to hurry." She lowered herself into the opening and slipped out of sight. There was a soft thud below.

"Do you see the Major?"

"He's out front, I think," she whispered.

Someone banged at the main hatch to the loft. I braced myself and swung down. The floor was a long way away, and it was bare earth, not straw. Horses' heads moved between the bars ringing the top of each stall. I let go, landing with a jolt that dropped my arches and flattened the heels of my sandals. Crystal eased the door open, then pulled back. The Major was returning. I leaned against the dark wood of the stall. A few seconds later, his trim head was silhouetted in the stall window. He was still smoking and seemed to be gazing out at the woods.

Crystal beckoned to me and crept through the door. I had gotten just a look at the rows of horse blankets and flysheets, riding crops and halters, when the groom came rattling down the ladder. I yanked at Crystal, but before she closed the stall door she hauled a boot with a heavy wooden boot tree inside. The groom passed us and caught the Major's attention.

"*Eh, bonjour, monsieur. Puis-je vous aider?*"

"*Bonjour,*" the Major replied over our heads. "*J'attende un ami. J'ai besoin de parler avec Monsieur Blythe.*"

"*C'est bien, monsieur,*" the groom replied. He resumed whistling, and the Major returned to staring at the trees.

Crystal lifted the boot and glanced toward the unsuspecting Major. I shook my head: perhaps he would take a stroll elsewhere. We waited for a couple of minutes, listening to the groom in the loft throw hay down to the horses in the stalls behind us, while the pungent odor of the Major's cigar permeated the stable. Then the door at the back of the building opened, and Edward's entrance sealed Major Smith's fate. Shaking off my hand, Crystal stepped toward the front of the stall, raised the boot, and cracked the Major on the back of the head. She slid the bolt and flung open the door, throwing him, stunned, to the walk. The weapon thumped on the gravel as she took off at a run, leaving the Major clutching his head and trying to rise. I saw a horse blanket hanging within reach, and, moved by cowardice or compassion, I ignored the club, heaved the blanket over him, and fled across the yard.

Crystal was considerably more agile than I, and she disappeared instantly behind a clump of trees. I went leaping into the long grass and bushes, caught my ankle, and pitched painfully over the seat and handlebars of a rusty bicycle. The collision set one of its tires spinning, and I lay tangled in the chain and crossbars, my shoulder bag hoisted on the hand brakes and my hair caught in some scrub roses. I scrambled up, exposing more skin to the mercy of the thorns and brambles, and turned to where I was sure a circle of grooms, gendarmes, and secret agents waited to arrest me. There was no one. Through the thin screen of leaves I saw only the Major — or rather the horse blanket — lying on the gravel. As I watched, it swelled and flapped its sides like a tartan manta ray. First the front and then the rear rose, and from out of its blue and yellow depths the Major began roaring in loud, profane French that brought Edward, two grooms, and a pretty child on a Shetland to his assistance. Hands trembling, I disengaged my slacks from the chain's oily embrace, untangled my bag from the brakes, and looked around for an escape route. The van was gone. I glanced at the treacherous machine at my feet. It was a heavy, three-speed, man's Raleigh, and, despite neglect, it looked sound. I picked it up, brushed some snails off the seat, and wheeled it through the thorns and vines to a riding trail. Then I hopped on, pushed the rusted gears to high, and pedaled over the soft, leaf-strewn path through the hot green Bois.

The bike was rusty, its tires mere strips of rubber, and the wretched machine found every stone, every stick, and every rut on the path. Within minutes I was dripping with sweat and completely lost. Finally I yielded to reason, stopped the bike, and assessed the situation. The map of Paris — that was the first thing. I remembered the Bois as a green lozenge on the left-hand side. I concentrated on the bottom of the lozenge with its Métro station. I knew that there were other Métro stops along the right-hand side of the park, but I had no desire to retrace my steps. The thing to do was to head south, whichever way that might be, and avoid the main roads, where my panicky imagination envisioned the Major's Mustang and Edward's Porsche racing in tandem to cut off my escape. I spent some minutes consulting the sun glittering through the lacy trees; then I put on my dark glasses, tied my hair in my scarf, rolled up my slacks, and remounted the bike. I would be less conspicuous pedaling at a sensible rate, I decided, but I soon found that only frantic efforts kept the bike going on the soft ground. At last, disgusted with the meandering trail and reassured by the indifference of other cyclists and riders, I took one of the paved roads and, watchful of each passing auto, made my way to the base of the enormous park. There I circled Auteuil, wheeled the bike along a narrow lane behind the grandstand, and finally ditched it in the shelter of a clump of evergreens. A hundred yards ahead I saw the curving ironwork of a Métro sign. I ran there, hurried down the steps, through the turnstile, and into the narrow, claustrophobic tunnel as a train approached. Covered with mud, hay, cement dust, and bicycle grease, I entered the safety of the Paris transport system.

# Chapter 9

By FIVE P.M., I felt as though I'd spent a week in a mad doctor's health club. All my muscles were protesting the invention of the bicycle, and I was badly in need of a drink — of anything. Nonetheless, I was satisfied. Crystal Blythe had a seat on a 747 leaving at eleven-thirty the next morning, Bertrand Gilson had the latest news on the Blythe heirs, and I had official commendations and a few free days in Paris. Reluctantly, I put self-congratulations aside to wonder whether Crystal had told me everything she should have.

Five-fifteen: the fat man seemed to be on the hotel desk twenty-four hours a day. He gave me a knowing smirk. "Subject returned at five-fifteen in a disheveled state," he'd report, and Major Smith would reconsider the incident at the stable. Fortunately, it wouldn't matter. Crystal would be gone, and we'd be innocently viewing fountains and paintings and objets d'art by the time he came sniffing around. I unlocked the door. Harry was sitting at the table by the window sketching an enormous bunch of roses, stocks, and anemones.

"Hi," he said. "Isn't this perfect for that new florist's layout?"

"What? Oh, yes, beautiful. Where did you get them?"

"I didn't. They're yours — a present from the contrite Mr. Blythe. Here's his card. He's not so bad," Harry continued as I opened the envelope. "We had quite a talk."

"When did he arrive?"

"He just left. I'm surprised you didn't catch him on the way in."

"Do you remember what time he got here?"

"I'm not sure, Sherlock, around four, maybe."

I nodded. "Smart boy, Edward."

"What's the note say?"

"He swears off absinthe. Did he ask where I was?"

"Sorry to disappoint you, but he didn't."

I sat down opposite him and kicked off my sandals. Harry turned a new page in his notebook and started scraping a stump of charcoal back and forth. After a few minutes he said, "You're a mess. What have you been doing?"

"Finding Crystal Blythe."

"Congratulations. You won't have to worry anymore about that Major, will you?"

"No," I said, heading for the shower, "not excessively."

I elaborated on that at dinner. Harry was upset, and we had a long, aggravating discussion about my future at New World. Discussion is too bland a word. Harry offered me good advice, advice that I disliked simply because it was what I already had in mind. Then, as usual, I found it hard to fight with him. Harry is genuinely unselfish, and if he didn't make me feel guilty every now and again I'd make a fool of myself over him every time.

As it turned out, Harry could have rested his case: things were not all wrapped up, settled and serene. We had no sooner returned to the hotel room than the phone rang.

"Hello?"

"Hello, Mademoiselle Peters?"

"Yes, who is this?"

"Gaspare," he replied, and before I could warn him that the phone was unsafe, he told me Crystal was gone.

"Do you know where?"

"No, mademoiselle. She left in a car with a young man about her age. Thin, tall, dark."

"French or American?"

"French — Alsatian probably. He came just after seven. I don't know how he knew where she was unless she called him. They talked for a while, and then she said she was leaving and would be back in a few days."

"She's a fool."

"I think I should call the police."

"What could you tell them? She went willingly, didn't she?"

"Yes, that's true. I'm sorry, I advised her not to leave, but she told me not to worry."

"I understand. Thank you, Gaspare. I'll see what I can do," I promised and hung up the phone.

"She's disappeared again?"

"Right. With Gabriel, probably. I'm going to see Edward."

"Why not call?"

"I'd rather surprise him." I picked up the car keys and my coat.

"Want company?"

"Company, not protection."

"I had a partnership in mind: Peters and Radford, Private Investigation," he said slyly.

"Complete discretion guaranteed?"

"Corporate malfeasance our specialty."

I smiled. A business investigation company was the substance of his advice earlier in the evening, although he had not suggested joining the firm then.

"I may break into his apartment if he's out."

"You go right ahead, dear. I'll drive the getaway car."

I tossed him the keys. As we crossed the lobby, I noticed that the fat clerk was already on the phone. It figured.

In a few minutes we had left the brilliant ribbon of the Champs-Élysées for the quiet, elegant streets of the eighth arrondissement. Edward's town house was dark, as were the houses on either side.

"This it?" Harry asked, slowing the car.

"Yes, but don't stop. Turn around. We'll park on that side street we just passed."

"Quiet for this time of night."

"It's a residential area — very classy. Can you squeeze into that space?"

"After driving the van in Washington, this is a snap." I took the flashlight from the glove compartment.

"Let's look for his car, first."

"Then what?"

"Find a way to get in."

We walked along the street beside the garden. An old wall, spangled with moss and lichen, extended from the rear of the house to join the neighboring property. There was a heavy green wooden door at this juncture, and Harry squinted through an opening in the warped boards. "I think there's a garage."

"Any sign of his car?"

"The garage is closed."

"This door has a nice solid lock, too."

Harry jumped up and touched the top of the stone wall. It was high, but not impossible.

"Lift me up," I said. "I think the back windows are the best bet."

With Harry's help I grasped the top, then he gave me a push, and I hauled myself up. At the bottom of the garden was a short drive to the stone garage. A lawn ran from there to a shallow terrace outlined in boxwood, which gave access to the house through French windows. Below me were espaliered fruit trees and beds of fragrant, waxy lilies. I swung over and dropped onto the soft earth, knocking over a large potted plant. I set it upright and listened: a cricket and the distant sound of a radio, that was all. I crossed the grass and checked the garage. As I had expected, the door was unlocked and the building was empty. I turned toward the house, and through the long windows observed the empty hallway and living room. I took a penknife from my pocket. The first pair of windows was locked and the sash was tight, but the living room set had only been closed. They opened easily, and I was about to enter when I heard a sound from the garden. I dropped behind the shrubbery, debating whether to hide there or escape into the house, when Harry came tumbling over the top of the wall to land on one of the potted geraniums in the border. He straightened the plants as I had and looked around anxiously. I heard footsteps in the street and motioned to him.

"Someone's coming," he whispered when he reached me.

"You have a right to be on the street. You've a guilty conscience already," I said lightly, but I wished he had stayed outside. I didn't want him involved.

"I'm afraid so. What are we looking for?"

"I want to know if Edward's disappeared, too," I replied as I stepped through the window. The living room had heavy curtains, which we closed before switching on the flashlight. A clock ticked noisily on the mantel, its brass pendulum a gleaming eye that surveyed us disinterestedly. I moved the beam across the wall. There were rows and rows of leatherbound books on art and drama, some poetry and philosophy, the usual sprinkling of cheap novels, and a surprising number of works on guns, explosives, guerrilla warfare, and revolutionary politics.

"An unusual selection," I said. A large oil of a rider taking a rail fence hung over one section of the shelves, and I took it down. The space behind it was crammed with political pamphlets.

"Maybe they're the ones he took from Crystal's apartment," Harry suggested.

"It's possible. Why don't you go through the desk?" I suggested and opened the double doors next to the bookshelves. They led to a dining room, a pantry, and a kitchen — Mathilde's domain. There was nothing around that shouldn't have been. I returned to the living room.

"Look at this." Harry held up a thick magazine. It contained careful scale drawings of machine parts that fitted together to form a large, lethal gun.

"What kind of magazine is this?"

"It's a catalogue for U.S. military hardware. With pictures, see, of pistols and machine guns and their parts."

"Not exactly what an aesthete like Edward would read, is it?"

"No, and it's not a newsstand magazine, either."

"Is it for ordering spare parts?"

"Probably, and it shows you how to fit the weapon together."

"Hardly top secret."

"Not at all, but an odd thing to have lying around. And it's the latest one, too." He pointed to the date.

"Uh-huh. Where'd you find it?"

"This drawer."

I shone the flashlight into the cluttered papers, then picked one up. "What's this?"

Harry held it under the light. It was a clear pencil sketch. "I'm not sure, but it's nicely drawn."

"Never mind that, let's see if it's in the magazine."

"It's some sort of sighting device. Maybe one of those new infrared things."

"What do they do?"

"They allow you to sight in the dark through the body heat of the target."

"Ugh."

"Not very sporting," Harry agreed.

"Wait, is this it?"

"No, but it's close. See, this is different." Harry showed me a small knob on the drawing.

"For a lightweight machine gun?"

"Right. One equipped for night attack."

"Let's hope Edward's living theater ideas aren't running in that direction."

"He could just be drawing the parts," Harry suggested. "Some of these would make effective drawings if they were arranged abstractly, like many of Ernst's or Picabia's works. He's very interested — "

"No," I said, remembering my conversation with Sybil. "Crystal's the one who draws. Her mother mentioned that she's a good painter."

"Oh. Shall we take this?"

"Yes." I folded it carefully. "Can you tear the page out of the magazine without loosening the staples?"

"I think so. The pages aren't numbered, fortunately."

"Good. It's less apt to be noticed. I'll finish searching through the desk, then we'll poke around upstairs." I thought about the fat man at the hotel; we didn't have much time.

When the desk yielded nothing else of importance, we turned off the flashlight and reopened the drapes. The garden was as quiet as the black marble stairs that wound in a sinuous curve to the second floor. The room overlooking the garden was, judging from its graceful floral prints and bare dresser, Crystal's. Her closet was empty except for two large suitcases. The middle room, darker and smaller, was decorated as a combination study and guest room, while the one at the front of the house was obviously Edward's. Harry closed the curtains, and I switched on the lamp by the bed. The closet doors stood open, and there was an untidy pile of socks and ties on one bureau, as if their owner had dumped them out, found those that matched, and abandoned the rest. A suitcase stood by the bed, and a rectangle indented in the rug showed where a smaller one had rested.

"Looks as if Edward's taken off," Harry remarked. He spoke in a normal tone, and I jumped.

"Not so loud. Yes, I think you're right."

Harry rummaged inside the closet.

"Just a minute," I whispered. "Did you hear something?"

He shook his head, but I felt the sickening, airless sensation of fear.

"Let's get on with this," I said finally. "We've got to find out where he's gone."

Harry returned to the closets, and I opened the drawer of the night table. There were a few paperbacks, cough drops, a couple of pens, matchbooks, and a girl's photo. I turned it over. "Love to Eddie from Missy" was written in a round, exaggerated hand. As I closed the drawer, I noticed a pamphlet stuck under the phone.

"Anna," Harry said in a low, urgent voice.

I heard it, too. I reached for the pamphlet, then flicked off the light. The flashlight lay on the dark comforter, its yellow beam casting a distorted golden circle on the far wall. Harry shut it off as a key turned noisily in the lock downstairs. I stepped into the hall. The front door creaked open, and someone entered the foyer. A pale cone of light swept over the banister, and a man tramped into the living room. I knew who it was; I could smell his cigar.

"It's the Major, alone."

"Where?"

"Living room. He's probably checking just as we are."

"Maybe we can get downstairs," Harry suggested.

"Not good enough. He mustn't know we're here at all. We'll use the wall. It can't be too far from the back windows."

Maybe the Major had given Edward that weapons catalogue, or would it surprise him, too? More lights went on downstairs, and in their faint reflections we groped our way into Crystal's room and closed the door. The rear windows overlooked the garden and the wall. The sill was miles from the ground and yards from the wall, but Harry, more athletic than I, pronounced it feasible.

"Hold onto the gutter."

"Let's hope he doesn't look out the window," I said. "He probably has a second man somewhere on the street."

"You go first," Harry replied nonchalantly. "You're just barely tall enough."

I clambered through the window and sat for a moment with my legs dangling above the garden like a timid swimmer confronted with a bottomless pool. Then I let myself drop, leaving parts of my fingers on the window frame and pieces of my slacks on the stones. My feet searched futilely for the top of the wall.

"Hold the pipe," Harry cautioned.

I edged hand over hand to the end of the sill and reached into space. The gutter was old and damp, and when I tested my weight, it protested this abuse with a thin, creaking sound. I was ready to pull myself back up and face the Major when Harry leaned out to help me down. I felt the wall with my left foot. There I wobbled back and forth long enough to see that the street was empty and that the light in the living room had just been extinguished.

"Hurry," I whispered. The gutter screeched, and Harry landed next to my hands.

"The Major's probably on his way upstairs."

Harry leaped off recklessly. I dropped beside him.

"We'd better get to the car; he's sure to spot the open window."

I caught his arm. "The back way. If he noticed the car, he'd have someone watching it."

We ran to the bottom of the lane and around the block. The upstairs lights in the house were on.

"He had a key, didn't he?" Harry asked.

"That's right."

"Odd, isn't it?"

Under a street light I examined the pamphlet I'd found in Edward's room. "Check the car while I have a look at this."

Harry sneaked around the corner. "There's a blue Mustang parked on the main street. Is it his?"

"Right, and there's a tall, seedy fellow hanging around?"

"He's sitting in the front seat, smoking a cigarette."

"His second in command — comes complete with silent tread and a thirty-eight. Do you want to do something satisfying and disloyal?"

"To Major Smith?"

"Uh-huh. Call the police."

"And report a burglary."

I nodded. "Your French is better than mine."

"All right. I'll phone from that café we passed."

"Let me have the car keys. If we're lucky, we'll be able to get the car, too."

Edward's pamphlet was a hotel and restaurant guide folded open to Strasbourg. Someone had asterisked the three top hotels and circled one. I had an idea that was where we'd find Edward. I slipped the pamphlet into my pocket as I walked toward the car. Harry returned from the café, and almost simultaneously I heard the sound of an engine and squealing brakes. I dashed up the street to our car. Ahead, the lights of a police van flashed across the houses. The Mustang started with a roar and took off. I jerked open the door of the rented car and turned the key as voices floated down from the town house.

"They're sure efficient," Harry commented as he jumped in.

"Good for us." I hit the accelerator. "That should keep the Major busy for a few hours at least."

"Where are we going?"

I handed him the pamphlet.

"He's been making reservations."

"That's what I think. It was on the table by his bed, under the phone. According to Gaspare, Crystal's friend is Alsatian, and the only thing Crystal knew about Gabriel's business was that he traveled to Strasbourg a couple of times."

"Worth a try. We could call and find out."

"Yes, but first I'd like to visit Tony. With Major Smith and his friend temporarily out of action, this would be a good time. I can drop you at the hotel, but I'm afraid the Major will be checking on us sooner or later. What do you think?"

"I asked for it, didn't I?"

"There's nothing much he can do but be a nuisance, so if you want to brazen it out . . ."

"No, no," Harry said a trifle sourly, "I've always wanted to be a fugitive from justice."

"Not justice, Major Smith, not at all the same thing."

Harry answered with a noncommittal grunt.

"Now about our friend Antoine." I made a few suggestions that I thought might appeal even to honest Harry. He absorbed them in silence, opened his street map, and directed me to Tony's apartment off the Rue Vaugirard. We wound through a series of narrow streets, around a tree-filled park, and past the building. I turned one extra corner and parked the Citroën next to a battered moped chained to a street light. "Remember, what we scare out of him now won't hurt us later."

"He's probably not home," Harry replied with discouraging hopefulness. We entered a narrow, stone-floored lobby and hiked up two flights. Half the hall lights were missing, and those that remained served only to conjure snaky shadows from the vaguely art nouveau banister. The walls were peeling, the doors were dark and battered, the floors creaked — it was a perfect spy's lair. Tony either had a hidden sense of humor or he took himself much too seriously. Harry knocked on the last door in the hall.

"Tony? It's Harry Radford." He hammered again.

The door opened, and Tony appeared barefoot in T-shirt and jeans. When he saw me he would have slammed the door in our faces if I hadn't squeezed past them both into the apartment. It was a bleak den with a low ceiling and dark paneling, but bare, neat, and clean. There was a bed, two curtainless windows, and an alcove closed off by a pair of shutters. I opened them to find a clean but chipped sink and a hot plate. On the opposite wall was a stainless steel wardrobe. The meager furnishings were pure urban decay. I sat down on the only chair and said, "You weren't up for a discussion the other night. Are you better now?"

"Oh, yes, thank you. Bruised ribs and four stitches in my head. It would have been worse if you hadn't rescued me," he said with a smile to Harry.

It didn't get him anywhere. Harry grunted and leaned against the door. "Anna wants some information," he said, and I was impressed. He'd remembered something from last year's wretched crop of gangster movies.

"It's all up to the Major," Tony said briskly. "I'm out of the picture. I'm packing."

"What a coincidence. Harry and I are leaving Paris tonight, and I need to know where Edward and Crystal are."

"I have no idea." He didn't seem surprised that the Blythes had disappeared. He was very sure of himself.

"Tony, tell me something. What did you do during those three years in Army Intelligence?"

He looked stubborn.

"Come on. That's not top secret. It's all part of your record."

He shrugged. "This and that. I helped plan war games. I kept charts."

"Charts?"

"Russian tank strength. That kind of thing."

"Don't tell me you made the models."

"No, usually I worked with bar graphs."

"Nothing else? Nothing" — I gestured at the dim, little room — "like this, for instance?"

"Not until the Major."

"You met him recently?"

"That's right. I mentioned that my dad thought he could get me a job at New World, and Major Smith offered to help out. Said he'd put in a word for me with some people he knew."

"And then he requested some information."

"Well, it was all security, you understand. I was glad to help."

"I understand, though I think it was a mistake to trust the Major, Tony. It's not smart to take that officer-and-gentleman business too seriously."

"You're wrong there. He's quite genuine. No doubt about that."

"I'm sure he is, but he's gotten you into a lot of trouble. Our friend Major Smith has a fairly intricate scheme running. He wants Crystal and Edward left alone, perhaps because he hopes to locate Gaby through them, and he doesn't want anyone else asking questions. That's fair enough. But then he does something strange. He lets one of his people clatter through the student quarter hollering as though the plague had struck and stirring up all kinds of trouble. Isn't that odd? And when that person gets found out and beaten up he doesn't even move him out of Paris. What do you think of that?"

"I'm on my way now," Tony answered, but he looked less confident. "And as you can see, nothing's happened to me in the meantime." He started edging toward a squat chest. Harry reached back, opened the top drawer, and came up with an automatic.

"Lot of those around nowadays," I remarked.

"Loaded, too," Harry said.

"That's mine."

Harry shook his head. "Anna and I are in trouble because of you."

"I need that."

"Damn right," I said. "It looks to me as if Major Smith has

set you up for some reason. Gabriel's friends don't like questions, do they? If I were you, I wouldn't waste any time in leaving Paris, especially since Major Smith was arrested tonight."

"You're kidding! What for?"

"Breaking and entering."

"They can't arrest him. They'll have to let him go. He'll have some sort of immunity."

"Your outfit's in bad odor at the moment, Tony. He'll get off, probably, but you might just be stuck here."

"I can take care of myself."

"How about a little help from your friends?" I took out a bundle of francs. "Go to Orly and buy yourself a ticket on the first plane out of France."

"And what do you want?"

"I want to know if Edward alerted the Major about Gabriel?"

"Edward? No, I don't think so." Tony was amused.

"Oh, then the Major has been keeping an eye on Gabriel and the Blythes for some time?"

"I guess so, but I'm not going to discuss it with you. If you want to give me the money, fine, but I'm not telling you anything more."

"Of course." I picked at the stuffing oozing from the chair, Harry looked out the window, and Tony sat on the bed and began winding his watch. "We know what the Major's after."

"Then why ask me?"

"We want to be sure: it's guns, isn't it?"

"Safe guess."

"I'll be more specific: U.S. Army experimental models, light-weight, equipped for night firing."

That brought a response. "How do you know?"

"A little more than a guess. And here's another. They're smuggled in from one of our bases in Germany."

Tony's uneasy silence suggested we were on the right track.

"Gabriel and his friends had received a shipment of guns — or gun parts — and my hunch is that Crystal or Edward tipped off the Major. I would like to know which one."

Tony started to answer, but Harry stepped away from the window and signaled us to be quiet.

"What's wrong?"

"The blue Mustang just pulled up."

"The Major?"

"No, his pal."

"You'd better get out of here," Tony warned. "Remember Major Smith's advice?"

"Yes, but I still need to know about the Blythes."

"I don't have the answer."

"I don't happen to believe you. Tony will have to come with us, Harry."

"Wait a minute, I'm not going anywhere."

Harry raised the gun deliberately.

"If you trust this guy you're more of a fool than I thought. Is there a back way?"

Tony wavered. "He'll come up the side stairs. If we go right out front we'll miss him."

I waited.

"He'll be here in a minute. We've got to hurry."

His voice rose, and I decided he was telling the truth. Harry opened the door. There was no sign of anyone.

"Hurry," Tony repeated. He made a nervous conspirator.

We ran down the creaking steps, through the smelly corridors, and out. As we passed the Mustang, the lights went on in Tony's apartment.

"Where's your car?"

"Around the corner."

"We just missed him."

"Lucky for you. Get in."

"Where are you taking me?"

"That depends on you," I said and started the motor. "Crystal's disappeared again, probably with Gabriel. Where are they?"

"I don't know. Let me out."

Tony reached for the door handle, but Harry stopped him.
"Sorry, Tony, but it's double or nothing. Tell us where we can find Gabriel and Crystal, and I'll drop you at one of the Métro stops and give you the money to fly home. If you don't, it's going to be a long, dangerous walk back from wherever we decide to drop you."

Tony protested these alternatives while I struggled with the geography of Paris. Finally I told him to stop whining and direct us out of the city, which he did, in his best tour-guide style, until we reached the Bois de Vincennes.

"If we go any farther, I'll have to take the train back," he said plaintively.

"You're not cut out for this, you know, Tony."

"I don't have a centime on me."

"It won't hurt you to walk — if you're careful."

"My ribs are sore."

"We're going to drive until you tell us where to look for Gabriel," Harry said.

There was an extended pause. "Will you give me the gun back?"

"Sure thing." Harry opened it and removed the clip.

"Strasbourg," Tony said, and I slammed on the brakes and swerved over to the curb.

"Strasbourg's a big town."

"The Major was watching a house in the old quarter. Near the towers. I don't know the address, but it's right on the river. La Petite France, it's called. Gabriel used to go there. That's all I know."

"Thanks very much." I opened my purse and handed him the money. "Take this, go straight to the airport, fly back to the States, and forget you ever met the Major. Don't go back to your apartment."

"But my passport?"

"Forget it. Say you lost it and ask the American consulate for help. Or call someone from New World to pick it up for you, but drop out of sight and stay away from your apartment."

Tony stood dolefully on the curb. "Do you have any Métro tickets?"

I found one. Harry handed him the gun and threw the clip out of reach on the sidewalk. Tony dived after it as we screeched away from the curb and headed east.

# Chapter 10

**We called it a night** when we reached a town called Sézanne between Paris and Nancy. We found a room, I called Strasbourg and Washington, and Harry disappeared. By the time I learned that Edward had reservations at a big hotel on the Place de la Gare and told Gilson that the Blythe heirs had both decamped, Harry returned, smelling faintly of Scotch and smiling for the first time that evening. He had acquired a couple of new maps, which he spread out on the bed with interest.

"You might have invited me along," I said.

"All they had was Scotch, you don't like that."

"Nice to be asked."

"Don't tell me the pro's in need of some fortification."

"I sure am. You even had me scared — did you study under Clint Eastwood?"

"Ernest Borgnine. They don't make them like him anymore."

"Well, you were very good."

"That's what I've been waiting to hear," he replied, taking a small bottle of cognac from his jacket pocket.

I started to laugh. "You are extravagant! Where did you get it?"

"Extravagant is right. I bribed the bartender. Drink up and be merry."

I found a glass, and we exchanged toasts. "Quite an evening."

"Nothing to it," Harry said casually. "Let's see, breaking and entering . . ."

"Kidnapping . . ."

"Carrying a weapon without a permit . . ."

"Enough to merit the wanted list. I'm sorry we didn't add auto theft, too."

"Why?" Harry asked.

"All we've done is delay the Major, not eliminate him, and we're traceable through the car."

"Tomorrow," Harry said. "We steal a car tomorrow." And he fell back on the bed and laughed.

*

We didn't steal a car, although as it turned out we should have. What we did was start early for Strasbourg through a dreary gray rain that let up a little by the time we reached the Place de la Gare, a cobbled oval with a parking lot and a bus terminus at its center, hotels to the east, the station to the west, and streams of weary travelers with backpacks and overloaded suitcases. We parked with difficulty and claimed our room, which proved to be a large, square chamber curtained and shuttered against the as yet nonexistent sun. I opened the drapes, windows, and shutters and looked out on a narrow street jammed with people buying pastries, bread, fruit, clothes, and groceries at shops that were little more than stalls. A few timid cars crept past, but they were clearly intruders, and the street had a festive air with the heavy smell of food and the cheerful sounds of vacationers speaking in alternating waves of French and German. It was the height of the Strasbourg tourist season.

Harry looked over my shoulder. "There's a bookstore up the way, the concierge said. I think I'll go buy a guide to this place."

"You might pick up some clothes, too. Do you have any money?"

"Yes, I changed some yesterday. What do you want?"

"A shirt, some underwear. I'm going to see if Edward is in before we try to locate the other two."

"What are you going to say to him?"

"I think it's time for a candid talk. However much Edward dislikes Gabriel, I can't imagine that he would want to cooperate with Major Smith. Not with all that money rolling in at home. If it's power he's after, he'll have plenty of that without any effort."

"You don't seem to think it's pure patriotism."

"No chance. I think Edward saw an opportunity to get rid of someone he didn't like and to frighten his sister. No more than that."

Harry left, and I dialed the hotel.

"Edward Blythe, *s'il vous plaît.*"

"*Un moment.*"

The manager checked the register and rang. Not surprisingly, there was no answer; it was already midmorning. I went down to the lobby and questioned one of the porters, who remembered that the young man with the white Porsche had left the garage about an hour ago. We had just missed him, but he was still registered; there would be time for him later. I returned to our room. Harry was sitting on the bed thumbing through a guidebook. The other man was sitting in the chair next to the wash cubicle.

Our visitor was dressed in a dark suit that emphasized his black hair and eyes, and although short, he looked strong and compact. His tanned face had high, prominent cheekbones and features of an unusual precision and clarity. He didn't move when I entered except to incline his head slightly. I saw then that his eyes were intelligent and suspicious, and I had the impression that they seized and filed my image instantly.

Harry rustled some booklets and said, "Someone to see you, Anna."

"André Pillot," the man said. "My credentials."

"You're very formal." I skimmed the documents and handed them back. Monsieur Pillot worked for French security.

"Monsieur Morret of the petro consortium in Paris has told us of your company's cooperation in certain security matters," he said with an excellent English accent, "so I am hopeful we can conduct our business in a civilized manner. And, of course," he added without attempting to hide the dry contempt in his voice, "we get too few Americans here in Strasbourg. We are working to enlarge our international tourist trade."

"Monsieur Pillot is anxious for us to see the sights," Harry remarked.

"You're not the only one. We've been overwhelmed with suggestions already, haven't we, Harry."

He nodded, and Pillot asked, "From Major Smith perhaps?"

"Major Smith takes an interest in tourism."

"My government is interested in Major Smith. Unfortunately, he has not seen fit to cooperate with us."

"That is annoying, Monsieur Pillot, but I'm afraid that neither Harry nor I has the slightest influence with him."

Pillot leaned back in the wicker chair, which made a brittle, rustling sound. "I would like to know," he said, "what Major Smith is occupied with at the moment."

"Monsieur Morret has no doubt told you why we are in France?"

"He told me that you claimed to be on holiday; he believes that you are on an assignment for your company. Our government does not care to have industrial spies operating in France, mademoiselle."

Pillot's touchy nationalism gave me my first idea of the morning. "Monsieur Morret guessed incorrectly. I'm here for New World Oil, but it's a personal matter, rather a sad business, in fact."

Harry put on his most serious expression. "Anna is helping out an old friend and benefactor," he said.

"Perhaps you could tell me about this errand of mercy," Pillot replied sarcastically.

"I'd be glad to, since you're a member of the French government." I emphasized his official connection. "As guests in your country, we don't want to have any dealings with Major Smith without . . . ah . . ."

"Our sanction, you mean?"

"Well, your knowledge, at least."

Monsieur Pillot nodded. I doubted very much that he was deceived in the slightest by all this courtesy, but it smoothed his feathers. Respect for the glories of France seemed the way to his ear, if not his heart. "That is prudent," he said.

"My business involves two young people. They have no father, monsieur, very little guidance, and, for better or worse, they are about to inherit an important interest in New World Oil."

"You are referring to Edward and Crystal Blythe?"

"Yes. It is my impression that Major Smith has entangled them in one of his schemes."

"Unfortunately, that is correct."

I nodded. "They are very young, you understand, and they haven't the experience to be able to cope with a man like the Major."

"We are sympathetic, of course," Pillot said sententiously, "but wealth and privilege, even American wealth and privilege, cannot be allowed to break French law."

"I couldn't agree more, but I wanted to make my purpose clear. I'm here to take the Blythes home. You may not know that there has been a death in their family, and under the circumstances, their mother wants them back in the States."

"And is that your only concern, Mademoiselle Peters?"

"Absolutely. I was asked to deliver those security memos to Monsieur Morret, but otherwise, Harry and I are just sightseeing and trying to arrange the Blythes' safe return."

"Yes, and yet, mademoiselle, you immediately employed a man called Antoine Fermine when you arrived. Fermine is an acquaintance of Major Smith's."

"I didn't know that at the time, and our Paris office probably didn't either. As for employing a translator, that was simple: my French is rudimentary."

Pillot looked as though that alone condemned me.

"And Monsieur?" He gestured toward Harry. "What is Monsieur's role in all this?"

"I was invited," Harry said, "for the trip."

"My boss wanted me to have company."

Pillot looked dubious, and Harry didn't help matters by glaring belligerently at him.

"I want to take the Blythes home," I repeated after a moment. "What do you want?"

"If I get what I want, you may have the Blythe children."

"Can you guarantee that?"

"You have the assurances of the French government."

It wasn't the moment for antigovernment sentiment. I swallowed my skepticism and said, "Fine."

"Major Smith was detained briefly by the police in Paris last night," Pillot said. "I see you're not surprised."

"I should think that the Major Smiths of the world risk arrest fairly often."

Pillot raised his eyebrows. "Smith is looking for something that I would also like to locate."

"What's that?"

"We've been trying to cut off the flow of arms to terrorist groups. Your country is indirectly the source, because many of these weapons are stolen from U.S. military bases in Germany and smuggled into France."

"Where does Major Smith come in?"

"That, mademoiselle, is something of a mystery. To the best of our knowledge, he has been attempting to trace the stolen weapons. Unfortunately, he is a difficult man to pin down."

"I can imagine." I gave Harry a warning look. "Harry is a good draftsman. He could draw a weapon that would interest you — if you don't ask any questions about it."

"Agreed. Monsieur?"

Harry hesitated, and for a few seconds I was afraid he would offer Pillot the drawing and manual page. Then he reached for his sketchbook. Pillot stood behind him as Harry sketched the gun sight from memory.

"This is accurate?"

"As accurate as I can make it."

"You saw this?"

"No, only a sketch of it."

"Anything else? Mademoiselle?"

"We think it's an infrared gun sight for a light machine gun."

"That is an American weapon. A shipment of them disappeared recently from the U.S. Army base in Offenbach, Germany."

"And Major Smith wants to recover them?"

"No more than we do. We know who's after them."

"Major Smith's in your way?"

"To an extent, yes. So are you, Mademoiselle."

"Escort the Blythes to a plane, and we'll leave today."

"That can't be done yet. They are under surveillance, and you will be, too. For your own safety, stay here and conduct yourselves like ordinary visitors."

"We've heard that before."

"But you haven't heard this before: Antoine Fermine is missing. We naturally suspect foul play."

"Why?"

"He left behind his passport, money, and clothes. And he's vulnerable because he works for Major Smith and may know about Smith's assignment. Perhaps, also, you and Monsieur have reasons for disliking him."

"You think we're responsible for Tony's disappearance?" Harry asked.

Pillot smiled. "Certainly not, but it would be easy enough to arrest you both on suspicion. So take my advice and be careful not to interfere in any way. If we find the guns and break up the ring transporting them, you two will leave France with the Blythes. If you get in the way, I will make life very unpleasant for you."

"I fail to see how we could interfere," I said.

"By taking the Blythes home before we give you permission. If you attempt it, I guarantee you will be arrested before you cross the border."

"If you don't trust us, you can arrest us now — if you can make the charges stick," Harry said gruffly.

"I can, but arresting you might alarm some of the people we're watching. Mademoiselle Peters and you have made your presence obvious."

"In other words, we're supposed to look the other way while you endanger Crystal and Edward. That's an awful risk to take."

"That's right, but you will cooperate because I can have you detained indefinitely." He folded Harry's sketch and went to the door. "Alsace is rich in art and culture," he said. "With any effort, you will enjoy your stay. Especially you, Monsieur Radford; our works of art are world-famous."

He left before Harry could suggest what he could do with his art.

"Where is the original drawing?"

"In my pocket. I almost gave it to him."

"That would have implicated Crystal or Edward. The less proof Pillot has, the better."

"Perhaps we should destroy it and the manual page."

"We may need it later. Crystal and Edward are not the world's most tractable people."

"Draw the curtains, would you?" Harry asked, shielding his eyes from the sun, which had finally vanquished the low clouds.

As I tugged the cord I noticed that the curtain lining was loose. "Here's the thing. We'll hide the drawing and the manual page in the hem." I smoothed the papers flat. "Notice anything?"

"No. How about when they're open?"

"Nope. Now watch the hotel send those curtains to the cleaners."

"Not this place," he said, swinging his feet onto the bed.

"What a mess we're in."

"Yeah, the firm's gone to hell since I joined. And I expected to keep you out of trouble."

"A nice thought, but overconfident. The only way we could have stayed out of trouble was never to have come."

"At least Tony seems to have gotten away clean."

"If we can believe Pillot."

"He's a cool customer."

"Very. And he knows a lot more than he's telling us."

"What are we going to do?"

"Just what the man said."

"We're giving up too easily."

"Maybe, but if Tony lives to grow up and sell T-shirts to tourists again, he'll have us to thank. Of course, we can't prove that. Over here you're guilty until proven innocent. Pillot could make a real stink if he wanted to. We were the last to see Tony alive, he left in our car, et cetera, et cetera. A little danger is one thing. Hanging around a French jail until Tony testifies that we didn't hurt a hair on his head is another."

"But it's ridiculous."

"Sure, but Pillot could construct a case against us if he put his mind to it, especially against you. I don't look substantial enough to have smashed Tony up, but, dear, in this country you look like John Wayne."

"Dubious flattery."

"Flattery or not, we're stuck. Besides, unless we turn up Crystal or Edward, we can't do a damned thing anyway."

Harry thumbed through his Strasbourg guide. "In that case, let's see the cathedral and drive down to Colmar. Now here's something," he said with a sly look. "I quote: 'One of the most interesting and best-preserved sections of old Strasbourg, with houses reflecting in the water of the canal.' It has fourteenth-century towers, too."

"Towers?"

"Yes, about four blocks from here. And guess what this well-preserved section is called?"

"I give up."

"La Petite France."

"That's the place Tony mentioned."

"And look at this." He pointed on the map to the bridges and islands in the middle of the river.

"That's very like what he described, isn't it?"

"Yes, and fourteenth century should make it 'rich in art and culture.' Pillot wouldn't want us to miss that. Shall we pay a visit to one of the quaint areas of old Strasbourg?"

"Definitely. You know, Harry, you're showing such persistence that I'm tempted to take your suggestion."

"Which one?"

"Peters and Radford, Inc. Investigations."

"Good, but just Peters, please. I'm retiring after this trip."

\*

Strasbourg sits on the Rhine in a mesh of canals and streams. The heart of the city is encircled by the narrow waters of the River Ill, and the stone walls bordering the streets along the water are broken by steps down to its weedy banks. These are the haunt of the city's fishermen, who cast from the shore or sit in narrow, flat-bottomed rowboats, of their dogs that hunt through the weeds, and of the tattered men who sleep in the odiferous shadows of the stone pilings of the bridges. Harry and I bought hot dogs at a stand on the bank, crossed the nearest bridge, and strolled along the quais. It was getting hot, and on closer inspection, the shores of the Ill had a dank odor. We climbed back to the sidewalk and admired the tall, narrow stone houses, the locks, the waterfall, and the first of the promised fourteenth-century relics, a square blackened tower that obstructed traffic at the corner of a narrow side street. Harry sketched while I watched the water and a pair of kids playing with a yellow dog, and tried to decide if the man in the gray workman's smock was following us.

"We can't be far from the house," Harry said.

"No. Are you finished with your sketch? The man behind us is beginning to think we're legitimate."

We continued along the curve of the river, past a parking lot that overlooked the locks to a series of little bridges. An immense building with a vast sloping roof and rows of tiny, widely spaced, barred windows dominated the opposite bank. This gloomy structure was a prison. On the other side, the Ill broke into four channels, and lining its banks were old stone and timber houses with their foundations almost in the water, their pots of pink geraniums and patches of white stucco reflecting in the weedy brown stream. The bridges were guarded by three medieval towers. Black, somber, and crumbling, they had loomed above the burghers' houses for six hundred years without losing their ominous appearance. Overhead, pigeons by the hundreds wheeled from their roosts in the towers and the vast attics of the prison, and every bench, cobblestone, and quai held white evidence of their picturesque, unhealthy presence.

"Not hard to imagine knights and robber barons here, is it?" Harry asked with satisfaction.

"Or beggars and thieves, either. It's pretty, but can you imagine the wintertime with all this water? No wonder they had plagues."

Indifferent to these medical reflections, Harry opened his sketchbook and drew the angular houses with swift, sure lines. I leaned on the bridge and wondered which house was Gabriel's and whether I could find him without drawing attention to myself. The old city along the water struck me as both charming and oppressive. The sun on the wood and stucco, the flowers, the birds, were charming, but the relics were grim. How many of Major Smith's ilk had perished in the service of the petty duchies of Alsace and the Rhineland, immured in towers like the black sentinels of La Petite France or caught too late in narrow, twisting streets like the ones threading the old town. Pillot had set my nerves on edge, even if he had failed to alarm Harry, and Strasbourg's dark canals and ancient buildings struck me as only too apt a metaphor for intrigue. Just then, a tour bus sporting a pink and white canopy rolled slowly past us, around the last tower, and up to a high platform over the widest part of the river. Harry glanced up from his sketch and said, "Look at that pretty girl."

I followed his glance. Several dun-colored houses with overgrown gardens rested on a spit of land jutting out into the Ill. From one of the houses a couple was walking toward the road. The man was slim, with dark wavy hair and fine pale features, and the woman was very blonde. I saw her face clearly as they stepped onto the asphalt. It was Crystal Blythe.

"That's her," I said in surprise. "That's Crystal."

"Who's with her?"

"Gabriel, I assume."

They stopped short, and I think Crystal would have bolted if her companion hadn't realized she'd seen us. He said something to her; then she waved, and they came over. Crystal glanced uneasily at her friend.

"Hello, hello." Crystal greeted us as if we were long-lost friends. "What are you doing here, Anna?"

I felt like saying, "You know perfectly well, you spoiled little idiot," but managed to hold my temper. "We're on our way to Colmar. Harry stopped here first to see the cathedral and these towers."

"Colmar is beautiful," Crystal's companion said eagerly. "I'm Gabriel Celestin." He shook my hand. "And you're Anna."

"Anna Peters. Nice to meet you."

"Crystal didn't tell me she was expecting friends," Gabriel said.

"It was a spur-of-the-moment thing."

"Do you live around here?" Harry asked.

"That was my mother's house." He pointed to an old building behind the tower. "The other one's empty. There's some talk of them being renovated. But when are you going to Colmar? This afternoon?"

"We're just about to pick up our car," Harry said. "It's not a long drive, is it?"

"What a coincidence," Gabriel exclaimed with a great show of enthusiasm. "We're heading there, too. The wine fair's on now, and they're featuring a Nashville group. Your country music is very popular in France. Here's what we'll do. We'll drive down to the museum, and afterward I'll show you the town — it's lovely. Then dinner at the Maison des Têtes — they'd like that, wouldn't they, Crystal? — and some country music at the open-air theater."

"Gabriel's too impulsive," Crystal said to me; I couldn't tell if it was a warning.

"No, no. How often do I meet your friends from the States?" he asked with emphasis. "They'd have a good time. Wouldn't you?"

"That's nice of you," Harry said, glancing at me to show he wasn't intimidated by Pillot.

"*Bon.* It's all settled, then. You don't mind?" he asked me casually. In spite of his enthusiasm, his eyes were cold.

"It would be a pleasure," I replied.

# Chapter 11

It was midafternoon when we reached Colmar, and the sky was hazy with heat. Gabriel directed us off the main road to a shady park with broad walks and an ornate fountain. People were eating ice cream and drinking beer on the terrace of a restaurant, while around the gravel oval in the center, children peddled wooden horses under the watchful eyes of their parents and the toy concessionaire. Beyond this green was a busy square, the Place Rapp, and off that, a quaint and pretty old town with ornate woodwork and narrow cobblestone streets where red and yellow pennants fluttered in honor of the wine festival.

"I wish I had my camera," Harry remarked.

"Oh, did you forget it?" Gabriel asked.

"No — that is, the shutter's sticking. I, uh, left it in Paris for repairs." Harry gave me a reproachful look, and Gabriel sympathized. He'd been friendly and informative on the way down, rambling on about Alsace and the Unterlinden Museum, and behaving in general like a man anxious to impress us. From behind the wheel I caught occasional glimpses of his greenish eyes. They never lost their cool reserve, not even when he laughed, and I was curious about what he was planning. Logically, he should have preferred to put as much distance between us and himself as possible.

"We ought to head for the museum," Crystal said finally. "They close at six."

"You must have visited here before," I remarked to Crystal. She and I were carefully sticking to neutral topics.

"Twice. Edward and I came about a year ago. The altarpiece is incredible. It's the greatest thing in Germanic art, absolutely."

"I've been looking forward to seeing it," Harry put in. "Do you paint, too?"

"I've studied for years," she replied. "That's about all my school taught, that and riding. Perhaps I'll decide to earn an honest living from art someday. Gaby would approve of that, wouldn't you, Gaby?" She was teasing, but her words carried a sting. Gabriel wisely refused to be drawn into a discussion.

"Don't be fooled by this guided tour of Renaissance Colmar," she continued, taking Harry's arm playfully. "Gabriel really thinks art is immoral."

"Immoral?"

"Art today doesn't serve the people," she intoned maliciously. "It is a parasite of the ruling classes."

"Crystal knows nothing about politics," Gabriel said to me.

"I think it's hard to understand another country's politics. Ours are complicated enough." Crystal and Harry walked on ahead of us. Crystal talked animatedly, and Harry stretched out his hands as though measuring the fish that got away.

"Your country's politics are easy to understand: what serves the interests of the major corporations is translated into national policy."

"That's true everywhere: economic interests are always important. They're probably the most important factors, but they're not the only ones."

"Everything comes from the economic structure," Gabriel said positively. He was dogmatic, and I understood why Crystal was tempted to needle him. He gave one an itch for disagreement.

"I find that odd coming from you. Crystal told me you were a poet, a writer."

"A poet is not necessarily a writer. There is poetry in action as well."

I thought about Edward: there must be something in the crystalline Parisian air. "American politics has been plagued by poetry in action. John Wilkes Booth, for instance."

"Booth?"

"The actor who assassinated President Lincoln."

Gabriel stiffened. "You have a violent country."

"You should talk. By your own account, this province hasn't exactly been a place of sweetness and light."

"No state ever has been. The state by its nature has a monopoly on violence, on approved violence. The United States is particularly violent because of its power."

"Violence in the population increases as the violence of the state increases? That's possible, but other factors can dispose people toward violence. And you forget where we are in history compared to Europe. Look at your religious wars, at the Thirty Years' War and Napoleon."

"That's why the power structure of the existing states must be changed. The energy of the state should be available to the people rather than to the hatreds of the establishment."

"You mean their self-interest."

"Their self-interest and their hatreds, yes. There are too many people, too few resources, and too much power to allow a handful of people to control the destinies of nations. Why don't people realize that? You. You're in business, Crystal says. Can't you appreciate the need for change?"

"Yes, but most people fear change. They prefer their current brand of misery to an unknown set of problems."

"Power ultimately resides in the masses," Gaby said, warming to the topic.

I was getting weary of his idealism and the ambition it concealed. "So does everything, corruption included. The old Calvinists were right about that."

"If you really believed that, you'd be religious," Gabriel said. He had very white skin, without color even when he was annoyed or excited, and beautiful hair. He was a romantic-looking young man who seemed destined to end up as a beautiful newsphoto.

"The trouble with revolutions is that they never end the way they are supposed to end."

Gabriel wasn't listening. He was talking about Camus, and 1968, and China. I listened and thought again about Edward, who hated him.

"Come on," Crystal called. "There's the museum."

"This time it must be different," Gabriel was saying.

"It won't be for you," I replied. "The poets are always the first to go."

"And you agree?"

"Oh, no, I'd keep the poets, but then I'm not in the revolution business. If you are, I'd advise you to prepare for a bad end."

"Hurry up, you two," Crystal urged, cutting off his reply. "This is rather pretty, don't you think, with the well? Gabriel ought to write more and talk less," she added, then she said something else in French that I couldn't follow. She seemed annoyed with Gabriel and yet protective of him.

He took her hand, and we followed them through the crowded, dark-paneled lobby into a series of bare, modern galleries installed around the courtyard of the ancient convent. The side galleries housed the lesser lights of the museum's collection: provincial artists' madonnas and martyrdoms, done with gold-leaf backgrounds, sumptuous brocades, and exquisitely detailed tortures. The virgins and saints were aristocratic and ethereal; their worldly tormentors, brutal and unredeemed. The artists shared a detailed knowledge of pageantry and atrocity, and I wondered what the men who limned those mutilations and dismemberments would have made of Gabriel's artistic theories — or of Edward's. Crystal laughed, and I saw her pointing to a rainbow-colored Saint Ursula.

"I wrote a series of poems about these paintings once," Gabriel remarked. "They didn't turn out well."

"I can't say I like the subject."

"Weak stomach?"

"I've seen someone burn to death. It's an experience that stays with you."

Gabriel looked up from the martyr's agony. "Oil worker?"

"Hired killer," I replied, and without waiting for another question, I entered the final gallery, where the enormous wings of the Issenheim altarpiece stood open, tourists and tour guides clustered where once the victims of medieval plagues had awaited miracles.

In front, visible from the whole extent of the old chapel, was the crucifixion, a gigantic, livid corpse spanning a vast and ominous night sky. Behind, an annunciation, a nativity, and a resurrection: all glowing in reds, golds, blues, and oranges, saints and angels vibrating in ecstasy. And last, the two panels of the patron, Saint Anthony: in one, serene in a fantastic landscape of greens, blues, and browns, and in the other, tormented by the putrefying demons of a dizzying witches' Sabbath. Altogether, they formed a most extraordinary set of images, with realism, mysticism, and fantasy coexisting harmoniously. This was the synthesis that had eluded the painters of those awkward, but richly decorated madonnas and martyrdoms in the other galleries: this perfect blend of degrading horror and ecstatic liberation.

Harry was staring in rapt admiration with Crystal beside him, while Gabriel examined the saints on the side panels. I had an odd, double sense of awareness: of the splendid, mysterious altarpiece and, simultaneously, of the four of us, and of the pattern of relationships, which was, for a moment, as bright, sharp, and wonderfully incomprehensible as the radiant designs that had burned on those panels for centuries. Then the perception faded, and I walked out onto the balcony overlooking the grassy center court, empty except for an old well and a couple of nondescript shrubs. The others were still admiring the Grünewalds and some smaller paintings at the far end of the hall, but I didn't want to blur the remarkable vitality and clarity of the images floating magically in my mind. Could this be what Harry perceived whenever he looked at pictures and objects? And did such bright, lingering afterimages enable him to remember what he saw, and later to transpose the memories into new patterns? I had a sudden insight into a different type of mind, and I was examining the idea so intently that I didn't notice Crystal until she leaned over the ledge next to me, breaking my train of thought and bringing me sharply back to present, practical problems.

"I love it here," she said, pushing her long hair back from

her eyes. In spite of the coquettish gesture, she seemed nervous and sad.

I glanced at my watch. "You should be beginning the descent into JFK. Why didn't you go?"

"I just couldn't, that's all."

"Because of Gabriel?"

"Yes, he begged me to stay. We've been quite close, you know."

"You told me before you'd gotten bored with changing the world through improved Maoism. Have you changed your mind again, or do you have a bad conscience about Gabriel?"

Crystal ignored this.

"What are you planning to do when he finds out about you?"

"The family, you mean? Oh, I don't suppose it will matter. I'm going home in a few days."

"That's not what I meant. Gabriel must have asked you along for a reason — as a sort of hostage, perhaps, or because he's suspicious."

"I don't know."

"Maybe he intends to find out if you're the one who steered the police in his direction. He won't be happy with the answer."

"I didn't!" She looked around quickly. "I didn't — it was all Edward's fault."

"Was it? Living with Gaby was chic and exciting until you got scared. You found out some things about Gaby you shouldn't have and told Edward. I'm aware of Gaby's activities, and so is the French government. He is involved in transporting stolen weapons, U.S. Army machine guns with ultramodern night sights. I saw the sketch in Edward's apartment, a drawing you'd made — it was you, wasn't it? — of a special gun sight?"

"Shhh."

"We're alone." But I was wrong. A woman was wandering along the exhibits of Alsatian ironwork and pottery that lay in the glass-topped cases overlooking the courtyard. Then Gabriel and Harry joined us.

"Do you want to see the Picasso exhibit?"

"Go ahead, we'll join you," I said. "Crystal and I are on our way to the washroom."

"We're going downstairs, too," Gabriel explained. "They've redone the crypt to make an exhibition room." He watched Crystal intently as he spoke.

"It's a lovely museum," Harry said, and we all agreed. We were getting awfully good at small talk.

Downstairs, except for the massive stone arches, everything was modern: functional design and indirect fluorescents for the relics of Roman and pre-Roman Alsace, for the traveling Picasso exhibit, and for the lavatories, which were tiled and furnished American style. Crystal sat on the counter that held the sinks and lit a cigarette.

"You'd better get away from him," I said when I was sure that we had the place to ourselves. She didn't answer. "How long do you think it will take him to guess that Edward's turned him in — if he hasn't guessed already? Edward, that is, with your help."

"It wasn't deliberate! Edward didn't believe me. I told him I wanted to go home, that I was in trouble. He thought I was kidding. So I drew the gun sight for him. I found it in some fishing tackle at Gabriel's."

"Fishing tackle?"

She knocked off the ash of her cigarette. "Yes. I was in the mood to go fishing one day, and I rummaged through Gaby's tackle box. There was a hunk of metal wrapped in grease and oilcloth."

"And that is what you drew for Edward?"

"Why not? We always confided in each other. And I assumed — well, Edward loves that kind of thing: mystery, danger, unsavory people — I thought that if I confided in him we'd be friends again. It never occurred to me that he'd hurt Gaby."

"Edward would forgive your desertion if you betrayed Gabriel?"

"It sounds stupid now, but I didn't realize how Edward had changed. I trusted him."

"I wouldn't waste time on regrets. Those are dangerous

weapons Gaby's fooling with. Their only purpose is to kill a lot of people. In all probability they would wind up in the hands of fanatics, who hope to use them as political muscle. But —"

Harry tapped on the door. "Anna? Are you in there?"

"Yes, we'll be out in a minute."

"I'm going upstairs."

"All right."

"Gaby will be suspicious." Crystal slid off the counter.

"You have sense enough to be afraid of him, but you didn't leave when I instructed you to. Here, take my car keys and drive back to Paris right now."

Crystal hesitated for a second, then shook her head.

"Is this to spite your brother, because he didn't believe you were in danger? It's a risky way to say 'I told you so.'"

"But you can't stop me," she replied and pushed open the door to reveal Gaby waiting impatiently outside.

*

The haze lifted around sunset, and when we came out of the restaurant, the sky was a clear, pale lavender, and the street lights and Colmar's bright windows shone green and gold against it. We lessened the effect of the fine Alsatian cooking by walking slowly back to the car, Harry and I strolling a little behind Crystal and Gabriel, lingering over façades and fountains and other evidence of Old World Charm. I'm glad we enjoyed the OWC, because I've remembered that pretty town as sinister ever since.

Then it was different. The evening was warm and pleasant, and I'd had enough *coq au Riesling* and the green-tinged wine that went with it to weaken my usual paranoia. Crystal and Gabriel — and Edward, too — were such unlikely conspirators. One equestrienne, one theatrical dilettante, and one poet-cum–Marxist revolutionary: they were not what I would have recruited. But one of them was smuggling stolen weapons, one was part of an intelligence scheme to retrieve them, and one had betrayed one or both of the others. The more I thought it over, the less sure I was that I'd figured correctly who was to blame for what.

"Gabriel certainly isn't up on country music," Harry said.
"Is that what you two were discussing on the way to dinner?"
"He's not familiar with Hank Snow."
"He's lucky."
"Don't be a snob. And he drew a blank on Hank Williams and the Wilburn Brothers."
"You sound surprised."
"I am, a little."
"My hunch is that Gaby's meeting someone at the concert. We're along for window-dressing."
"And then?"
"Then he cuts out."
"As a partner in this firm I'm entitled to advise."
"Okay."
"When we reach the car, grab Crystal, get in, and take off. I'll handle Gabriel."
"I've already tried to persuade her to leave."
"She doesn't have to agree."
"And we'll have another kidnapping to our credit. Also, you're forgetting Pillot."
"Scratch plan one."
"The most we can do is to stay close to Crystal."
Gabriel opened the rear door for us. "Shall I drive? It's a tricky route."
"Is it far?"
"Not at all. Just outside of town. There's a hall for the wine tasting, an open-air theater, and a cabaret. We'll be in time to see some of the dancing. The fair is pretty at night."
"Hank Snow," Harry remarked to no one in particular, "is the grand old man of the Grand Ole Opry."
"Ah," said Gabriel, "perhaps he'll come to France one day."
Gabriel was either remarkably complaisant or endowed with wonderful self-control. If we or Major Smith or French security or his own group worried him, he gave no sign of it, and within ten minutes he had driven us to the fairground, a field lit by strings of bulbs hung between the trees and by the yellow glow of the *halle aux vins* and the dance hall. Music issued from the

latter, a series of American tunes rendered almost unrecognizable by the characteristic rhythm of French pop, which, to my ears at least, transforms everything to Muzak.

"You ought to taste some of the young wines," Gabriel said as he parked.

We all protested that we had drunk enough already.

"*Quel dommage.* I'll come back after we get our tickets," he remarked and led us to a wide, fenced oval that held seats and an open stage separated by a second fence from a good-sized crowd. The crowd was equipped with autograph books and cameras, and it was being amused by a Bluegrass group that sounded authentic until the vocals began. We bought tickets and sat down, half-blinded by the alternating bands of glare and shadow created by the high floodlights. When the local aggregation finished the set, Gabriel announced that he was going back to the *halle aux vins.* I waited until he reached the gate, said I had to visit the ladies' room, and squeezed down the row before Crystal could decide to accompany me. I spotted Gabriel's white shirt as soon as I got outside the fence.

The fair seemed to have become more crowded in the brief time we'd sat in the theater. Latecomers hurried up to the ticket windows; girls with long skirts and platform heels teetered beside their escorts; cheerful, red-faced tipplers discussed the young wines. Someone was playing an accordian at the edge of the crowd, and softened by distance and the damp night, melodies drifted from the dance floors. The early reports predicted that the new vintage would be a success.

I lost Gabriel for a moment, walked faster, and picked him up again. I wasn't too worried that he'd notice me. In his idealism, his composure, and his moody self-absorption, Gaby struck me as intelligent but not alert in a practical sense. He moved purposefully through the crowd, and as he neared the first building, the cabaret, I closed the distance between us, afraid of losing him in the mob milling before the doorway. He turned the corner; I stopped so quickly I almost tripped. Around the building came a cloud of strong blue smoke and a long cigar. At the end of the cigar was Major Smith.

"Good evening," he said, and like a fool I nearly answered him when another male voice replied, "Well, George, what are you doing here?"

I retreated behind the building, around a wooden fire escape, and past a collection of trash barrels to emerge on the other side of the cabaret. The Major and his friend were casually eyeing the local color. They didn't convince me. I raced across the sidewalk into the neighboring *halle aux vins,* an exhibition room, tavern, snack bar, and dance floor, which was hot and noisy. Gaby was not there, nor was he among the group that had spilled from the hall to dance in wide, slow circles on the grass, spreading out from the source of the music like the waves of sound pulsing between the trees. Cautiously I retraced my steps and hid in the crowd until I was sure the Major had gone. Then I went into the cabaret. Tables and chairs lined the walls, but everyone seemed to be dancing, and the smoky air was laced with laughter. I thought I spotted Gaby's light shirt far to the rear before I was caught in the throng, which spun like a carousel, its centrifugal force sending couples from the middle of the floor to the edge and back in long loops.

A man with a broad smiling face, a flashy pink shirt, and a gold medallion wrapped both arms around me and whirled me half off my feet. He spoke in German and laughed. He had two gold teeth, a bushy mustache, curly brown hair, and a neckline plunging to his waist. He smelled of beer. I said in French that I was looking for a friend. He laughed again, and I realized he was cold sober. I gestured toward the exit, but he had a good grip on my waist, and my right hand was covered by a mass of red knuckles. He was an energetic dancer, fond of sudden swoops and changes of direction. On one of these forays I saw Gaby dancing with a dark, chunky young woman, and when the music changed tempo, as it did periodically, he released her and hurried toward the back of the cabaret.

My partner pulled me closer as if to improve our acquaintance. I located his ankle and gave it a good kick. As he hopped in the middle of a complicated step, I slipped from his grasp to push between the nearest couples, knocking a wineglass off a table in the process. I didn't apologize. Sidestepping a waiter, I ran for a narrow hallway and out the rear door. I crossed the grass toward the spot where I'd last seen the Major, but dazzled by the brightness, my eyes registered only the fading green ghosts of the cabaret lights until someone moved from the shelter of the wall and blocked my way. His rather dreamy, abstract air was gone: Gabriel Celestin was all business.

"Not a music lover, Anna?"

"Let's say I prefer the real thing."

"Why did you follow me?"

"Same reason you invited us."

Gaby grabbed my arm. "There's no time," he began, drawing me toward the shadow of the building. "It's important that —" He broke off and turned at the sound of footsteps on the walk.

"*Pardon!*" A figure spoke in the darkness. "Ah, Gabriel and Anna! *Bonsoir,*" said Edward Blythe.

He was immaculately dressed, as usual, in a pale gray-blue suit, and our stunned silence did not disturb him. "I thought I saw you near the theater. I've had a time catching up with you," he finished with a dazzling smile.

Gaby remained silent. For him, Edward could only mean trouble.

"Did you see Crystal?"

"No! Is she here, too? At the theater?"

I nodded. He was a natural.

"I'll come with you. It's been a while since I've seen my sister. I haven't exactly been her favorite person lately, but I'm in luck now, because she behaves very well in company. And we have something to celebrate, don't we, Anna? Bad of you not to inform me; Mother called with the news. I can't imagine what happened to her letter, can you? Don't feel left out, Gabriel. We'll all have a drink later, and I'll explain. My sister doesn't tell you everything, I'm sure."

We returned to the open-air stage. I had expected Gaby to

excuse himself and leave, but I hadn't considered his formidable sangfroid. Edward bought a ticket at the gate, and we took seats behind Harry and Crystal just as the first set began.

"Hello, Edward," Crystal said sulkily in return to his greeting. She turned toward the stage and began chewing on her lip.

Her brother smiled maliciously and settled down to gaze at the stars, serenely ignoring both his companions and the music. The rest of us concentrated on the stage show until intermission, when Edward suggested getting something to eat. Since, for different reasons, we were all intent on keeping up appearances, we took up this idea as if we had nothing on our minds but food and music. Finally Crystal and I convinced Edward that we didn't need another dinner, and he offered to buy everyone some wine.

"Where's your car?" he asked casually.

"Where is it, Gabriel? It's a few blocks that way, isn't it?"

"It's down on the main road."

"You should have put it in the lot," Edward corrected. He was the type who always finds a parking space.

Gabriel was unperturbed. "You can give us a lift back."

"Sure. You want a drink?"

"Gabriel's been to the *halle aux vins* already," Crystal warned.

"No more for me."

"Sure?" Edward asked. "Well, why don't you get my car, and we'll meet you in front in a few minutes. You can't miss the car; it's right on the corner at the near side of the lot."

"You must have arrived early," Crystal said, but her brother ignored her.

"All right," Gabriel replied.

"Oh, don't be so lazy, Edward," Crystal protested. "We'll all go, Gaby. We're not in a rush."

"It's no bother," Gabriel replied.

Edward handed Gabriel his keys. "We'll wait for you over by those trees."

"You could have gotten the car yourself," Crystal complained after Gabriel left.

"I want another drink," Edward said. He gave me a sly look. Crystal caught it, too.

"I'm going with Gabriel."

"Come on," her brother coaxed. "He enjoys driving. Don't make such a fuss. Now, who wants what?"

And for the second time that evening we debated our plans, while Crystal tried to keep Gabriel in sight.

"I'll buy a couple bottles of wine, and I want a pizza. What about you, Harry?"

"Nothing, but I'll help carry the wine."

They went to the *halle aux vins,* and Crystal wandered restlessly outside. As soon as Edward and Harry returned, she headed toward the parking lot.

"This way, Crystal. I told him we'd meet at the corner."

"He's not there," she replied angrily, and despite Edward's warning that we'd miss Gaby, we trailed down the slope to the parking lot below.

"Is that him?" Harry picked out a light shirt a hundred yards ahead.

Crystal called, but whatever had detained Gaby earlier did not delay him now. He sprinted across the dirt road to the Porsche, its enameled skin shining like fresh milk.

Nearby, a car pulled out of one of the rows and accelerated on the access road. It was moving without lights, and when the driver suddenly switched on his high beams, they blinded Gabriel. The car surged forward, and we watched, horrified, as Gabriel dived toward the Porsche. The car swerved. Headlights raked the row of parked cars and Gabriel, his arms stretching for safety. I heard a thud and the sound of shattering glass. Gabriel was flung into the air, above the car hood, and Crystal's scream cut through my head like a knife. The driver slammed on the brakes, reversed the car, and stopped. He jumped out, saw us, and got back in. The tires scattered dirt and gravel as the car tore through the lot to the main road.

Gabriel was lying by the Porsche, one hand on his chest, the other flung toward the keys winking in the dirt just out of reach.

His head was twisted at an odd angle. Crystal reached him first and dropped beside him. His eyelids twitched.

"Don't move him," Harry warned.

Gaby's eyes opened at the sound, and he stared straight at me, his eyes dark.

"*Dites* Pillot," he said clearly, "Strasbourg." He shivered slightly, his eyes closing. Crystal felt for his pulse, then rested her hand on his chest, but Gabriel did not respond. Blood began oozing from the side of his mouth. Harry touched his face, then lifted one of his eyelids.

"Is he all right?" Edward asked, pushing Harry aside and kneeling opposite Crystal. "He's alive, isn't he?"

Gradually I became aware of voices above us on the slope and of people gathering along the road. Crystal glared at her brother. "You killed him," she whispered. "You knew they'd be waiting. You killed him."

"Are you crazy? I don't know anything about this. Believe me, Crystal, I don't —"

"Don't lie to me!" Her voice rose to a scream. "They're your keys, aren't they?" She scooped them up and hurled them at Edward. "You wanted him dead. You killed —"

Edward slapped her so hard that she almost fell over. Harry grabbed him, and I had to restrain Crystal, who was crying and screaming at the same time, from rushing at her brother. "Get the police," I appealed to the people surrounding us. "*Les gendarmes, les gendarmes. Ce jeune homme est mort.*" Crystal shouted something in French, and I shook her violently and yelled at her to shut up before she had us all arrested.

There was a long, awful silence before people began asking questions, talking all at once in an attempt to ignore the body sprawled before us. Edward, his voice trembling, explained how the accident happened, and I led Crystal to the edge of the crowd and made her sit down. A portly man carrying a leather bag arrived, and, just as he started examining the body, two motorcycle policemen, who waved us all away.

# Chapter 12

In the confusion caused by the accident, I left Colmar. The police were absorbed in measurements and photographs of the body and statements from Edward and Crystal. They were not yet curious about the observations of English-speaking foreigners, and after a word to Harry, I slipped back to our car. No one was watching. The show was over, and the principal actors had left the theater without taking their bows. It had been a provocative performance, and had Gabriel not revealed his disguise at the last moment, the dénouement would have been sad but simple: would-be revolutionary, betrayed by lover and/or rival, is killed by suspicious comrades. A familiar political tragedy.

The headlights made iridescent halos in the mist, and as I raced over the unfamiliar road to Strasbourg, I thought about Gaby and the Blythes. The parking lot and Gaby reaching for the car keys. So Gabriel had worked with Pillot. I'd missed that, but I still had a pretty good notion of what Gabriel had learned. He'd discovered who was smuggling the guns into France. And finally I knew the answer, too, because only one possibility made sense. Only one person could have profited from the bizarre sequence of events, beginning with Tony's clownish attempts at undercover work, and only one person was capable of murder. That person was Major Smith.

What was his game? His job, patently, was to recover the weapons and prevent future thefts. But he'd been sloppy. In fact, if he had deliberately set out to muddle the situation, and to throw everyone on both sides into confusion, he could scarcely have done better than to introduce a pair of oil heirs, a fake disappearance, and a blundering phony like Tony Fermine.

Gabriel's death, assuming as I did that the Major was ultimately responsible, clinched it. It makes no sense to kill off the middleman if you are hunting his contacts at both ends of the trail. The middleman is eliminated only out of stupidity, and the Major wasn't stupid, or out of fear, and the Major had not struck me as cowardly. No. Gaby was eliminated because he had learned something crucial. Something he had no doubt substantiated during our trip to Colmar.

The tires screeched on a sharp turn, and I realized I was driving much too fast. What was it Pillot had said when we talked about Major Smith? "We know who wants them." So they hadn't known the source. The weapons came from one of our German bases. Gaby must have confirmed which one. And who had stolen them. The Major had to shut Gaby up — or else he'd have been implicated. It was the only explanation.

The lights of Strasbourg rose ahead, a glittering choker above the black velvet décolletage of the Ill. I eased up on the gas as I passed the hospital complex and crossed into La Petite France at a decent speed. I was certain that Pillot had left someone watching the house on the river, so I turned at the first of the square towers, drove over the bridges, and parked in the lot above the river where the islands of the old city ended with Gabriel's dun-colored house and its forlorn garden. A few lights were sprinkled across the upper floors of the houses; below them, the cafés were dark. I took the flashlight and walked across the first bridge to the base of the tower that almost blocked the pathway to Gabriel's house. I waited for a moment, surprised at the silence, and tried the door to the tower, but it was secured with a lock that might last have turned a century ago. A few yards away the river glistened under a cloud of mist, and beside it a narrow path ran past two boarded-up houses before ending at the third. I pushed open the rusty wire gate to the garden and stopped again. I didn't like the fact that I hadn't been challenged. Pillot's men should have been there. Had I guessed incorrectly? Had Pillot himself gone to Colmar? A faint odor of smoke hung in the air, but in the misty night I couldn't see which chimney was smoking. A light glimmered in the house before me. Maybe Pillot had stationed someone inside. The front door swung open. I wrapped a handkerchief around the flashlight and switched it on. I was in a kitchen that had an unkitchenlike smell of lubricant and cigarettes. There were dishes on the rusty sink, a few bits of string and tape on the table, and several boxes stacked underneath. Probably Gabriel and his friends had stored the gun parts here.

I hesitated for a moment, sensing someone, but was unable to distinguish any sound or smell or movement to substantiate the impression. Clever, cowardly instinct warned me to leave. I shone the flashlight through the doorway, into the hall and living room, obtaining a glimpse of water-stained walls and a sagging couch. Stepping into the hall, I touched something that made me jump back and almost fell over a dark bundle on the floor. My heart raced, but the bundle was warm, alive, and securely bound. Pillot had stationed a watchman, all right, and he'd been knocked unconscious. Setting the flashlight down, I tugged at the knots binding his wrists and heard a footstep on the stairs too late. The windows were shuttered, and by the time I retreated to the kitchen, Major Smith was already on the landing. He aimed a pistol at me, and he didn't seem like an Old Boy at a reunion any longer. He looked damned dangerous.

"Stop right there, Miss Peters. Put down the flashlight. And now upstairs, please. Are you armed? Let's check. A stupid omission, I'd say. Straight ahead. I'm finishing a little chore, and I'm afraid I can't allow you to interrupt me. Right in here. The first door."

A fire blazed in the fireplace. The Major swept some sheets of paper into the fire with his foot.

"By the window, Miss Peters, but don't touch the shutters."

I obeyed. The room was small and square, with a double bed, an armoire, a chest, and several stacks of books. I surmised that they were camouflage for the gun parts, destined for the bookshop in the Latin Quarter. Across the hall, a similar room was lined with shelves. The Major knelt by the fire and fed the remaining papers to the flames.

"There now. A pity your sex's vice is curiosity. I trust you've satisfied yours, Miss Peters." He straightened up and raised the pistol.

"Almost." The Major was in a hurry; I, on the other hand, felt irresistibly inclined for a chat. "So Gaby kept records. You took a big chance coming back here, didn't you?"

"Not as much as you did. I had a little housekeeping to attend to."

"Gaby's death will cost you plenty. The government won't be satisfied with nabbing a few gunrunners now. They'll track you down until they find you."

"The charge would be manslaughter, and I didn't run over Gabriel Celestin."

"No, but you set it up — with Edward's help. Or did Edward understand what was happening?"

"Edward's been useful."

"I'm sure. And you nearly brought it off. You almost managed to sell those weapons, catch the people who bought them, and get away clean. Too bad Gaby turned out to be more than just an idealistic amateur. It must have been a very profitable racket."

"I ought to have gotten rid of you in Paris, but believe me, it will be well worth doing now."

"You've waited too long," I said quickly. "Strasbourg is crawling with agents. Killing me won't improve your chances."

"You're wrong there. The city is full of radicals, Miss Peters, militant radicals, and outsiders get hurt. That's what's going to happen to you. And isn't that more plausible than any other story? It's a calculated risk. The Blythes were a complication, but as things turned out, they distracted attention from me. Perhaps your death will do the same."

"You're an optimist."

"No, but I believe in gambling, as you do. How did you decide that I and not Gabriel's friends was to blame?"

"Just a guess. Nothing added up otherwise."

The Major hesitated, assessing this information. "Well, it doesn't matter. One phase of my career is over in any case," he sighed, fitting a silencer to the muzzle of the pistol. For the first time it hit me that I might not escape. Like most people, I have a strong conviction of my own immortality. Death always happens to someone else — someone unlucky, like Gaby — not to me. My throat went dry. Not to me! I stepped back involuntarily. I couldn't speak, but my mouth opened, and I must have screamed because Major Smith seized my arm, to use me as a shield. A high, metallic sound echoed below, and it forced the Major to forget everything but his own safety. I could hear my heart and his breathing, then a noise under the window and people in the kitchen.

"Stay where you are," the Major yelled, "I've got Peters."

I imagined a consultation below to tote up my value — tactical, diplomatic, security. I bit my lip and tried to collect myself. The main thing: the Major must believe that he can get away. Otherwise, he'll kill me. I tried to control my breathing. Count one, two, three, exhale.

"All right, Major, come on down."

"Get everyone out of the house, Pillot, and behind the fence."

Silence, then, "Very well." I couldn't judge the number of his men by their footsteps. Four? And one outside made five? Enough to separate me from the Major?

"Downstairs," the Major said.

He must think he has a chance. He must think —

"Walk slowly." He shoved me. "And no sudden moves, or you're dead. Do you understand that?"

"Yes." It was someone else's voice. I was surprised to find that my legs still worked. The Major followed. Downstairs, the lights were on. The hall was papered in a gloomy greenish brown. The stair carpet was torn. A clock ticked. One, two, three, inhale. The varnish on the banister was sticky. We stopped at the bottom of the stairs. The living room was empty, although a shadow streaked across the window.

"Get them away from the windows," Major Smith yelled so suddenly I jumped. The kitchen looked smaller than it had by flashlight. Odd how ideas take shape. The Major's scheme might end this way, with someone shot next to a dirty sink while armed men stood outside.

Pillot shouted orders in French.

"When we get outside, if Pillot's men are behind the fence, start toward the road, slowly. Follow the path along the water. If anything happens — even the slightest slip — I'll shoot."

I nodded. He had the gift of clarity.

"Good. Open the door."

I did. The desolate ark of the prison stood on the opposite bank; the potential jailers leaned against the fence.

"Clear this side," Major Smith commanded.

Pillot hesitated until I was sure my luck had run out, then waved his men away. The Major said, "Now," and we started toward the tower. A man aiming a rifle appeared on the parapet, and I hoped he had his orders straight. Beside the path the long grass was wet, and our feet made a swishing sound. Halfway to the tower. Fear acts like a magnifying lens. The sound of the river. The damp, ethereal breath of the mist. The cigar smell clinging to the Major like a bad reputation. Insignificant details became palpable. The Major's Mustang was parked next to an old garage. Two men reclined against the hood, and our procession halted. Pillot jerked his head, and they backed away. Major Smith handed me the car keys and instructed me to drive. His automatic brushed my ear as I slid behind the wheel. Four French agents arranged themselves in a gloomy semicircle around the car; the others ran to their vehicles.

"You're crazy."

"Not with this car. It's a custom job — four-fifty engine, ratios all changed. It'll do a hundred and fifty miles per hour easily." He rested the barrel on my neck. "I trust you're a good driver."

"I'm no Janet Guthrie," I replied, starting the engine. The agents scattered.

"They'll be right on our tail. We must make certain they don't trail too closely because I need a minute or so on them. I'll direct you," he continued in a precise, pedantic voice, "and as long as you obey my directions, you won't get hurt."

"Where to?"

"Go right, then left and a right. That'll put us on a main street. Move it!"

We bounced out of the lot and onto a cobblestone street no wider than an alley.

"Fast," said the Major, and I accelerated, spinning the wheel so that we squealed around a sharp corner and onto a chute where the houses hugged the road. The headlights flashed across the wood and stucco façades, a gate, and picked up a solid stone wall. I hit the brake and felt the machine slide toward annihilation before the tires caught and the headlights revealed another twisting lane and street lights ahead. The Major glanced behind us. "Faster." The beams of the pursuing cars wavered in the rearview mirror like eyes. I slowed automatically as we approached the main street, and the Major cursed. Buildings, storefronts, parked cars, a passing truck; I floored the gas pedal and the Mustang took off with alarming power. The speedometer leaped to fifty and climbed steadily; when it passed ninety, I ceased checking.

"A hundred and twenty will beat them," the Major observed laconically.

I swerved around a slower car, sending the Mustang into the wrong lane as the speed distorted my reactions. I twisted the wheel sharply; the car wobbled, then swerved into the right lane. Strasbourg's gray buildings flew by, borne on the noise of the wind rushing through the open windows, and I began to experience the odd, dizzying fascination of speed, the sudden vertigo of destruction. Red light. The brakes screamed, then the Major, and I felt the muzzle again. The cross-streets were a horror: a slow-moving produce truck, a cyclist, a sports car that missed us by inches. My hands ached from gripping the wheel, and images of torn metal and burning gasoline flared in my mind each time I slammed on the brakes or the Major yelled "Faster." We hit the curb once and almost turned over; after that I found myself able to concentrate. I blocked out the Major's automatic, the lights, and the cars tailing us to focus on the instant, on the slightest turn of the wheel, on the precise sound of the machine's acceleration.

"Turn right over this bridge," the Major barked.

I lifted my foot from the gas pedal, and the car slowed into the turn. We raced through the intersection and onto a wide, modern boulevard. There was room to maneuver, and the road was straight and open.

"Where are we going?"

"Straight, goddammit. Give it more gas."

I pulled out to avoid a truck and hastily back to miss a passing car. "You'll get us killed," I said, and then it occurred to me that the Major had given me a weapon quite as lethal as his own. "I can't control the car at any higher speed."

He looked over my shoulder. "They're dropping back," he observed with satisfaction.

"They can radio ahead to set up a roadblock."

"I only need a moment," he replied. "Right turn." It was a rotary with traffic lights and two cars blocking our lane. The speedometer dropped until I wasn't afraid to consult it.

"Drive around them!"

I swerved into the oncoming lane, saw the car, hesitated, then floored the accelerator, threading the gap.

"Faster," the Major shouted. The car lunged forward. "Right, turn right."

The rails of another bridge whipped past; we were heading for the Port du Rhin.

"We're in the clear."

The car shivered like an animal and pressed us back against the seats. Warehouses, silos, grain elevators, trucks, loading depots, merged into one monstrous, intricate structure. The docks loomed in front of us, their cranes like praying mantises.

"Left at the next cross-street. Left!"

The streets in the port area led nowhere. They dead-ended in parking lots and unloading stations.

"Where to?"

"Faster," the Major said, wagging the gun. "Here's where we lose them."

We roared down a long straightaway. The lights behind us were pinpricks, tiny and remote. Far ahead, the access road bent into a sharp turn.

"Slow down at the corner to let me out."

"No way."

The Major waved the gun.

"Put that away," I said. "At this speed you'd be committing suicide." My hands felt slippery on the wheel.

"Take your foot off the gas."

"They'll catch us."

The Major grabbed my shoulder, and the Mustang swerved. He released me and leaned back in his seat. "You'll never survive a crash at this speed," he said. I had to admit he was a cool customer.

"I wouldn't survive a bullet at this range, either."

The buildings loomed ahead at the sharp dogleg in the road. Better to take my chance with the Major.

"Don't be an ass. Slow down and I'll jump out."

"And you'll shoot me as I drive away. No witnesses, right?"

There was a silo and a derrick. It wouldn't be long now.

"You're hysterical. I'm not going to kill you." His voice was loud above the motor.

"Unload the gun." My heart was pounding.

"You're crazy."

"You have another gun, don't you? You asked for a minute; you've got it. I want fifteen seconds or so. Unload the gun or we crash."

Derricks. Windows. Silhouettes of warehouses. They grew bigger, and the walls at the corner became sharp and inevitable.

"The brakes!" the Major shouted, and the clip rattled to the floor as I lifted my foot from the gas pedal. "It's empty. Here!"

The weapon slid along the dashboard as I hit the brakes. The car veered to the right. Steer. Brake again. The warehouses and grain elevators rose up to meet us. I could see the cables on the derricks. We were going to crash. The Major fumbled for his other gun.

"Keep your hands on the dashboard!"

The car left rubber all over the road. Too late. The speedometer dropped — seventy, sixty-five, sixty. The Major braced against the door, whispering obscenities — fifty, forty-five — headlights bouncing off the mortar. The tires screeched. Too late. The cement blocks leaped up, large as houses. Thirty-five, thirty — wall head on, too late.

"Turn, turn, you stupid bitch, turn!"

The car slid toward the wall while the speedometer sank. We bounced against the curb. The warehouses spun past us, and the Major leaped from the car. Before me, the road lay straight for several hundred yards toward a parking lot. I jammed the gas pedal and ducked. The first shot must have gone wild, but the second shattered the windshield, and the third hit a tire. The Mustang wobbled out of control. I pumped the brakes and stumbled out as soon as it rolled to a stop. The night was quiet, and there was no one around to see me standing chilled and trembling in the middle of nowhere. Then I heard the police cars and a moment later I was transfixed by their beams. I raised my hands and edged away from the Mustang.

"Where's the Major?"

I pointed to the dogleg. One of the police cars took off while Pillot used his radio to dispatch cars and searchlights and agents to the warehouses where the Major had disappeared. A helicopter, too, because shortly one hovered over the canals that led from the Rhine to the docks.

"We'll get him sooner or later," Pillot announced.

I shrugged. The Major had already gotten more time than he needed. But that was Pillot's worry. Mine was legs that had turned to mush. I sat down at the edge of the road on the pavement littered with stones and broken glass. Pillot was impatient to whisk me away for a serious talk, but I sat down anyway. It had been a long evening.

# Chapter 13

HAD MAJOR SMITH BEEN FOUND that night, would everything have been different? Perhaps what happened was inevitable, and if the Blythes had been whisked home, back to the life they'd rejected in Connecticut, events in Strasbourg would simply have occurred elsewhere. I suspect that's true, though I'd prefer to think that nothing is predestined, that incidents, however logical and consonant with personality, may to the last minute be altered. If only this or that had been different. If Major Smith had been apprehended, for example, or if the Blythes had returned to Paris.

But Major Smith remained free, and Harry, the Blythes, and I were sequestered in Strasbourg. Our presence was testimony to the impotence of the secret service. As the Major's escape began to look more permanent, Pillot and company busied themselves with assigning an assortment of schemes to Smith and with rounding up various troublemakers who might know his whereabouts. Futile as this campaign seemed, its upshot was plain and simple: we were detained.

Supposedly we were detained because of the tragedy in Colmar. A more important reason was Pillot's desire to learn how Gabriel's cover had been blown. The real reason was that our government could not, or would not, produce Major Smith. So after a lengthy interrogation by Pillot, we were lodged in a comfortable old house off the Place Kléber, our passports were collected, and we were forbidden to go out unaccompanied. Pillot referred to this arrangement as "precautions." Since he declined to remove the Blythes to the greater safety of Paris, I termed it "harassment." In any case, no one was eager to secure our release, and in the gloomy aftermath of Colmar, we seemed unable to exert ourselves. Harry was allowed to spend afternoons along the Ill coaching one of Pillot's men who was an enthusiastic amateur painter. Crystal went shopping with a grim-faced lady whom she called "Agent X." I spent a long time on the phone to Washington, pleading for our deliverance, and even more time with the two New World lawyers who had been shuttled from Paris. Instead of harassing the French authorities about our detention, they pestered me about legal negotiations with the Blythes. Edward was another recipient of their unwelcome attention, but aside from listening halfheartedly to their proposals, he was lethargic. He drank in the dining room until Pillot locked up the liquor. Then he stayed in his room.

On the surface, Crystal and Edward seemed to have been reconciled. There were no more arguments or accusations, and there was no repetition of the unpleasant evening Harry and I had spent with Edward in Paris. They were quiet and subdued, as befitted the circumstances; they showed no excessive emotion. Far from affecting their lives deeply, Gabriel Celestin might never have existed. His death seemed to have signaled the end of an evil spell. Most people would have accepted the Blythes as a pair of innocent, charming, beautiful young people, possessed of a heartless self-absorption.

Most people would have been wrong. I was, although I had had hints enough and although I was uneasy as well as troubled by both Crystal and Edward. They had, however, schooled themselves to conceal or distort their emotions, and if their education in other regards was sadly irregular, as actors, their native talents insured success. They fitted the roles they strove to create perfectly. Gabriel, their friend, their enemy, was dead, and they might be to blame. Yet they seemed devoid of feeling. After the initial shock of his death, they swept away the broken pieces, and within a few weeks they would amuse themselves with other affairs. In my opinion, their wealth and selfishness enabled them to carelessly erase a disastrous mistake. Because I resented that, I suppressed things I knew about the Blythes and minimized incidents that reminded me of their complexity, like the conversation I interrupted the afternoon the lawyers arrived.

For several hours that day I had tried to convince the New World representatives that there was no chance the Blythes would agree to let trustees administer their fortune. The twins were obviously intelligent and independent, and I doubted that they would ever relinquish control over their shares. I didn't add that I thought the Blythes were power-hungry or that the manipulation of companies would be the most challenging game of all for them. I merely suggested that the lawyers were wasting their time. No, no, the men in the double-knit suits argued, the twins were too young, their shares too important. If I had New World's interests at heart, I would somehow persuade the twins to allow Gilson and the other trustees to maintain financial control. "All for their own good, of course, Miss Peters."

I promised to think it over and showed them out. As I started back to my room, I heard Edward and Crystal arguing. Through the double doors of the living room, their voices were harsh and strained with anger.

"I've got to know," Crystal demanded. "I've got to know for sure."

"I've explained to you; we've gone over that. How many more times — "

"And I don't believe you. You never — " Her voice dropped and the words became indistinct, as did Edward's reply. Then there was a sudden, sharp sound that might have been a slap — or a book slammed on a table — and I opened the door.

The room was warm and dim, and the white afternoon light glittered in thin bands across the shuttered windows. Edward and Crystal stood at the far end of the room. Crystal declined a greeting and began twisting the curtain rope. She was wearing the monkey pendant I'd seen in her jewelry box in Paris, and I was about to end the silence with some comment about the pendant when Edward asked, "A rope to hang me with, Crystal?" Then, he addressed me with his usual banter. "Are the company wizards rescuing us?"

"The lawyers? Their main concern is business, I'm afraid. I just told them that I doubted you two would consider their proposal until you can leave Strasbourg."

"Damn right."

"They should send us home," Crystal added. "I'm sick of this place."

"You never know what might happen here, do you?" Edward's voice had a sour ring and a faint threat, too.

"Tell those creeps we don't care to see them again."

"Okay."

"When we get home, we'll have our own lawyers," Edward reminded his sister.

"When and if." She stalked out, slamming the doors.

"Things will never be the same." The anger drained from his voice. "We don't understand each other anymore."

He made me impatient. I recalled his behavior in Paris and the violent quarrel Jared mentioned. "Whose fault is that?"

"Oh, you're all on her side." He thumbed through a magazine, and his protective shell descended. He began to chatter about the lawyers and his latest fantasy: that Pillot was really a KGB agent. I laughed then, but it struck me later that Edward's clowning concealed a devastating shock. I should have understood him, actually, because his reaction to Gaby's death was a magnification of my own. Since that night at Colmar, Harry and I hadn't been able to joke about the situation, and humor was the weapon we had used against past difficulties. Like Edward, I caught myself musing whether our lives could be put back together on the old footing or if painful events and awkward compromises had dissolved intimacy. Gaby's death touched us, too, and reasonably or not, I blamed the twins.

That's why, when Harry tapped on my door later, I thought first of us, and only secondly and grudgingly of the Blythes.

Harry sat on the end of my bed. "Did you know Edward's been out?" he asked.

"You're not in your room, either," I said lightly. There were five rooms on the floor. We each had our own, one of Pillot's men occupied the fifth, and there were two bathrooms: Crystal and I had one, and Harry and Edward shared the one between their rooms with the agent.

"Be serious. I mean outside. There's a fire escape next door, and he climbs from it onto the roof and back through his window."

I remembered the fire escape at our hotel in Paris. For all his elegance, Edward was athletic. "Did you say anything to Pillot?"

"I think we've interfered with their lives enough."

"He'll have to be told. Edward probably goes out for a few drinks. Suppose some smart reporter gets hold of him — or worse yet, one of Gabriel's crowd? Pillot will have a fit, and I can't blame him."

"They should be sent home."

"What do you think I've been telling Pillot and the New World lawyers? But our government is stalling on the Major, either to save face or to kill a scandal, and so here we sit in retaliation."

Harry ignored me: people interest him more than politics. "There's something the matter with Edward," he said, "and with Crystal, too. I don't know what the hell they're trying to prove, but the act they're putting on can't last. It's unnatural. Too much has happened to them, no matter how they try to ignore the fact. I don't believe they're as superficial as they pretend. Something's got to give, and I don't particularly care to watch when it does."

"Edward may have a conscience after all," I said dryly.

"What about Crystal?"

I was unsure about Crystal. She showed more emotion but ultimately revealed less. "At least she's not out getting drunk."

"That's true. I wonder how much they blame themselves for Gabriel's death."

I had no answer. We sat in the darkness and listened to an

orchestra play old waltzes of regretful gaiety. When the music stopped, I made an effort to resume my responsibilities. "Has Edward returned?"

"Yes. That's what reminded me to tell you."

"I'm glad you did."

"I'd like to have a talk with Edward before we see Pillot. Do you mind?"

"No. Don't hope for too much."

"Do you think he's responsible for what happened?"

"I don't know. He wanted to get rid of Gaby, until he understood what that entailed. There's no doubt in my mind that he hated Gabriel, more than Crystal realized. He couldn't stand living without Crystal, yet he was jealous of her, the worst possible combination. It's ironic, though. He probably brought Gaby to the Major's attention as a gunrunner, but the Major had Gaby killed because he wasn't the genuine item. Does that implicate Edward?"

Harry sighed.

"I suppose there's enough guilt to go around. The Blythes should have known better in the first place. They got involved out of frivolity and arrogance."

"And we're innocent bystanders?"

"Yes," I said, "unless we're to be the civilian casualties."

"Sorry," he said gently. "I don't even like to think about the other night with the car."

"I'm not referring to that; I meant what can happen to you and me."

"That's why I feel sorry for them, though I don't much like either one," Harry said reflectively. "Events can change people, can change how you feel about people, even when nobody's at fault. They were as close as people can be, now they're strangers."

That bothered me, too, when I let myself consider it. "It's not wise to be so dependent on someone," I said. "That's one difference between us and them, but having to make a choice isn't always so easy, is it? One can choose not to bother."

"Is it a bother now?"

"Of course not."

"Not for me, either, though I wondered if you felt I'd failed you in some way."

I held his hands. "No, not in any way."

"It's awkward, though, Anna."

"Would you feel differently if it had been your job that got us into this predicament?"

"I suppose. I feel I should have, well, kept you from getting hurt."

"But you see I'm fine. And don't forget, things would have been worse for me without you. What bothers me is that I've mixed up the different parts of my life. That's stupid."

"You were aided and abetted," he said.

"Will things be the same between us when we're home?"

Harry assured me that they would, but later I woke up with nagging doubts. The curtains were blowing in the night breeze, and a full moon was shining.

"Edward? Edward?" Crystal whispered.

I sat up. My door was ajar, and in the faint light of the hallway Crystal appeared.

"Edward?"

"What's the matter, Crystal?" I asked sharply.

"Edward isn't in his room. I thought — "

I didn't appreciate her thought and was glad that Harry slept soundly. "Just a minute."

I got out of bed and pulled on a robe. "What time is it?"

"About three. I couldn't sleep, and I went to see if Edward could spare some sleeping pills."

We crossed the hall, and she opened Edward's door. His room was empty, the bed made.

"Have you checked downstairs?"

"He's not there. I've searched everywhere. He's been out all night. We must find him."

"I'll wake Harry. You get Pillot's guard."

"They don't have to know."

"Don't be silly. How will we get out?"

"Through the window, like Edward."

"Edward, but not three of us. And suppose some of Gaby's contacts are still in Strasbourg? We'll need help. Now wake the guard and ask him to call Pillot."

"But if Edward's all right?"

"If the worst that happens to Edward is a tongue-lashing from Pillot, he'll be lucky," I said impatiently and went to rouse Harry.

"Harry? Harry, wake up. Edward's gone."

"What time is it?"

"Three-ten."

"But I heard him in his room."

"He must have left again. Don't worry about it."

We were summoned to the living room when Pillot arrived. He was clean-shaven and as neatly turned out as ever, but there were dark patches under his eyes, and he seemed worried. "Ah, mademoiselle, monsieur. Sit down, please. Mademoiselle Blythe has informed us of her brother's absence. This is most serious." Pillot's assistant wilted unhappily under his sharp gaze. Crystal lit a cigarette; the blue smoke hung before her face like a veil.

"Monsieur Radford, your room adjoins Edward's. Can you tell us anything?"

"Edward climbed out his window earlier in the evening," Harry said, "but I was certain he returned around midnight. I must have been mistaken."

"You knew he left, yet you said nothing about it?"

"We're not in jail."

"Monsieur," Pillot began, but I interrupted.

"Do you have any idea where Edward is?"

"Mademoiselle Blythe has suggested a café in La Petite France. I have sent two men to check."

"He might be anywhere, of course," Crystal said.

"We could all help search," Harry offered.

"We will leave that to the police."

"I disagree, Monsieur Pillot," I said. "We're not under house arrest, and we don't need passports to walk around Strasbourg."

Crystal jumped up and jabbed out her cigarette. "That's right, and I'm going out, with or without the rest of you."

"You would do well to reconsider," Pillot advised. "Your brother has been involved with dangerous characters, as Mademoiselle Peters can testify."

"Will you drive us to the café or shall we take a cab?" Crystal asked.

Pillot hesitated. I had the impression that he wasn't totally displeased, that he was playing some game of his own. "Get the cars," he ordered his subordinates. They hurried downstairs, and we followed Pillot to the curb.

"It is a pity that I was not informed at once," he complained to Harry. We piled into Pillot's Citroën and headed toward La Petite France, the two agents following in the second car.

"Damn it all," said Harry.

"It's not your fault," Crystal said. "He's been drinking a lot, that's all."

"If you had any suspicions, mademoiselle, you should have informed us."

"You should have sent us back to Paris."

Pillot switched on his radio and called to the men he'd dispatched to the café. Had he hoped to lure someone out of the woodwork, or had he simply trusted the Blythes' lethargy and frivolity to keep them out of trouble? The transmitter squawked: Edward had left the café several hours before. "At closing," Pillot translated for us.

"When was that?"

"Around one."

It was four o'clock. We drove along the river to the lot where I had parked on the evening Major Smith and I took our joy ride. Tonight there was more moon and less mist, and the silvery Ill reflected the scattered, whitish clouds as flat, milky bands.

"The café's over there." Crystal pointed across the street.

Pillot tapped his manicured nails on the steering wheel. "Is there any reason he would visit the Celestin house?" he asked.

Crystal shook her head.

"We will look there first anyway," Pillot said. He issued orders on the transmitter. As we got out of the car, Pillot waved an assistant after us, then he swept his flashlight over the ground like a movie usher. I stopped when we passed the tower, certain Edward wasn't in the house.

"Let's walk around," I said to Harry.

Pillot's assistant trailed after us.

"What's up?"

"My hunch is that when the café closed, Edward went elsewhere for a drink."

"I sure wouldn't pick this setting if I were loaded."

"Me neither." We circled the dark tower and headed for the main road. This was the route the Major had used to leave La Petite France. Our feet crunched over a gravel lot bordering the bank of the river. Half-timbered houses occupied the far shore, a couple of flat-bottomed fishing boats tethered at their front doors.

"It would make a beautiful etching," Harry observed. He nodded toward the masses of the bridge and the tower, their darker shadows, and the subtle, luminous surface of the water. He added something about medieval proportions, but I was too nervous to pay attention. While Harry lectured the agent about art, I walked quickly along the bank.

And then I saw it. The crystal caught the light as the water did, despite its black onyx backing, and the gold chain winked in the moonlight. Behind me, Harry and the agent reduced the world to two lovely dimensions. I bent down as if to adjust my sandal and picked up the pendant. I'd seen it twice before and could not mistake it. The elegantly engraved little monkey sat in a spidery clump of bamboo, and on the back I felt the letters of Crystal's name. I had a sudden intuition of disaster and stuffed the pendant into my pocket.

"Find something, Anna?"

"Stone in my shoe," I replied.

The agent had reached the narrow bridge leading to the center of the city when he called, "Monsieur Radford, mademoiselle!" and switched on his flashlight. Half-hidden in the shadows were stakes or pilings set just before the bridge. The waters of the Ill eddied there, and the current had abandoned a large object against the stakes. The agent raised his flashlight: it shone on blond hair and a light shirt half-submerged in the black river.

"Oh, my God! It's Edward!"

The agent passed his flashlight to me and reached into the water, but Harry had already kicked off his shoes. The current lifted the body slightly, leaving a trail of white foam against the shoulder, and Edward's profile emerged for an instant. Harry splashed into the water. The Ill was deeper than we expected, for it rose above his chest instantly. The agent steadied him with one hand and shouted a stream of directions in French, until Harry freed Edward's body and floundered against the current to the shore. Finally the three of us were able to pull Edward from the water. There was a strong smell of slime and mud and weeds, and when I touched his arm, his flesh was cold. He had no heartbeat, and water poured from his mouth when I turned his head sideways.

"He's dead."

"He may not have been under long. Lift him onto the bank," Harry yelled. We dragged Edward's body onto the gravel. I could smell the river.

"I'll have Pillot call a doctor," I said, running toward Gabriel's house as Harry and the agent worked frantically to revive Edward.

"Pillot! Pillot!" The agent watching the cars stopped me. "We need a doctor. *Un médecin pour Edward. Tout de suite!*" I pointed to Harry and the agent kneeling beside the body. The man raced to his car, and I headed past the tower and along the narrow path.

"Pillot! Crystal!"

The door opened. "Not so loudly, please, mademoiselle. The neighborhood must not be aroused."

"We've found him!"

"Where?"

"The river."

Crystal came out of the house. "What's happened to my brother?"

Pillot pushed by me.

"Where's Edward?" Her voice was high, despairing. There was a chance that I was wrong. "Where is he?"

"Get hold of yourself. There's been an accident."

She started toward the road, but I put my arms around her shoulders. "Stay here, Crystal. It'll be better if — "

"Edward, Edward," she screamed, twisting away from me. She was strong, strong enough, I realized in a wave of nausea. Yet she was almost mad with grief.

She leaped up the slope to the road, her long fair hair flying, then gave another heart-rending scream that blended into the cry of the ambulance swerving through the narrow streets toward us. I chased her, out of breath. When I reached the bridge, I saw the circle of men around Edward, lights blinking on in buildings across the river, and Crystal racing down the path, her white blouse and slacks clear against the men's dark clothes. She broke through the circle, and for a moment there was no sound but her voice. Then they pulled her away from the body. By the time I reached them, she was sobbing in Harry's arms, and an agent was covering Edward's face with a jacket. I stood nearby, fingering the monkey pendant in my pocket.

# Chapter 14

THE AMBULANCE TOOK EDWARD'S BODY to the morgue, and we got Crystal back to the house on the Place Kléber, where the doctor insisted that she be kept under sedation until she could leave the city. She departed the next evening for Paris in a phalanx of police and New World Oil lawyers. Her mother, meanwhile, was in a Connecticut hospital in a state of hysterical collapse, and New World started shaking heaven and earth to get Edward's body shipped home and to protect Crystal like an empress in Paris. The official heat shot up like a blowtorch, and Pillot, the U.S. consulate, the commander of a certain American military base in Germany, and I all felt the blast. The others deserved it, in my estimation, but there was some feeling that New World's special investigator ought to catch hell, too, so I did not accompany Crystal to Paris. That was just as well. Crystal Blythe possessed a strong sense of self-preservation, and as soon as she had regained her composure, she wisely developed an aversion to my company.

"You understand, the events of the last few days — well, they're associated in her mind, you know, with, uh — "

"With me," I said. "It's perfectly natural."

The lawyer in the double-knit suit wiped his neck. He was an ex–football player who was converting muscle to fat, using business lunches as the catalyst. The humid heat of Strasbourg did not agree with him.

"Glad you understand that. We're leaving tonight," he said in a brisk, authoritative voice. "I told Pillot it had to be done. This whole thing's been mishandled from top to bottom."

"It certainly was a mistake to allow the twins to be kept in Strasbourg."

"As I mentioned to the home office when we were sent down

here, the company should have put those kids on a plane home right away."

"Oh? Did you? I was under the impression that you and Mr. Morby were quite content to leave the Blythes here, where they might be more amenable to your business proposals."

"That's a complete distortion of the facts! I can appreciate your desire to shift the blame for this fiasco, Miss Peters, but face it, you've screwed up."

"That's one way to look at it, Mr. Unwin, but I hope you've saved copies of your cables to Mr. Gilson and the consulate. I have mine, plus my notes covering the two discussions I had with you and Morby."

"Your organizational skills are well known," he said. "I'm not referring to that. Morby and I wouldn't say anything against you in that regard, but two deaths — that's terrible! Dynamite in the wrong hands! Can't screw up worse than to lose the client, can you? So, you're smart to cover your tracks. Yes, sir — yes, ms. I should say."

Unwin was a comic, but he'd have worried me if I hadn't been on the phone to Gilson — on his private line. No one knew about those calls but me.

"Edward's dead because he was poorly protected in spite of my protests. Neither you nor Mr. Morby chose to support me, and I would appreciate it if you would stick to the facts."

"You don't need to get pushy. That's what's wrong here. Can't push the French. No way. Finesse with them. You take a blunt approach, scream when you should whisper, and you get nowhere. You haven't been over here long enough to know how to handle them, but Morby and I know you never take the frontal approach, you've got to slip it to them sideways. Take your time, let things develop. That was our approach, and if this tragedy had been averted, you'd have seen the results."

"Mr. Unwin, you and Morby may take any approach you wish, but you are not to talk to Crystal again about any of the trustees' proposals."

"What do you take me for? The kid's in shock!" Unwin was

horrified, but his briefcase was bulging, and it wasn't with lunch, either.

"As of today, I've been authorized by Bertrand Gilson to secure an agreement with Crystal, and I will do that, Mr. Unwin, in my own good time, without any assistance from you or Morby."

"Not so fast. The Paris office — "

"Don't argue with me and forget the Paris office. Call Washington and speak to the chairman of the board if you want confirmation. If I find out that you and Morby have bothered Crystal — "

"You'll be lucky if you still have a job after this mess," Unwin interrupted.

"Maybe, but don't count on it."

Unwin checked his digital watch to show me he was a busy man. "We'll be leaving in a few hours with Miss Blythe. I have a lot to do in the meantime."

"Don't let me detain you," I said. He left later without saying good-by.

So did Crystal. I watched from the window as Agent X, two burly policemen, and Unwin and Morby escorted her to the limousine. In her plain, dark dress she looked young and fragile, and she held the agent's arm as if she could guess what lay in store for her. Pillot had a final word with the driver before they pulled away into the twilight. I stared out the window until the car disappeared, then went next door to Crystal's room and threw open the shutters. The bed had been made, by Agent X probably, but Crystal had left behind unopened shopping bags and the stack of tops and slacks that hadn't fitted into her suitcase. I was to pack these, and later Pillot and I would go through Edward's possessions before they were shipped home.

I opened the bureau and the closets, but the only item of interest was a pair of slightly damp and very dirty sneakers. They proved nothing except that Crystal was untidy. I wrapped them in plastic and put them in my own suitcase, anyway. Crystal — and Edward, too — had had the time and opportunity to dispose of anything they wished kept secret. I had unfolded the garment bag Pillot had sent up and had begun packing when the breeze from the window slammed the door against the outer wall with a bang that made me jump. Damn! My nerves weren't made for this life. And then it struck me. When my door opened, it creaked like the portal of a dungeon in a Frankenstein movie. Yes, and Harry's door, too. The hardware on the Place Kléber was antique, and it made standard Gothic mansion noises. I shut the door: not a sound, although the hinges were old. And oily. Fascinating. The doorknob turned quietly, and I noticed faint sticky patches above and below the latch. Puzzled, I stood at the window for a moment, watching the sky fade to gray. The bureau? A roll of thick adhesive tape. I hadn't paid any attention to it. Crystal had no cuts or sprains. What else do you use tape for? I took the scissors from my room and taped the latch: the door opened and closed soundlessly. This discovery was as disturbingly suggestive as the monkey pendant. I decided that I ought to test Edward's door. Fortunately, Pillot hadn't locked it. The latch clicked softly. No creak, no groan. I switched on the overhead light to examine the door. Its hinges and lock had been oiled as well.

I opened the shutters for a breath of air. They made a considerable clatter, and almost immediately Harry appeared.

"Anna, it's you! I heard the shutters and wondered who in the world was in here." He looked around sadly. "Funny what you think of sometimes." He thumbed through one of Edward's books, then set it down with a sigh. "I wish like hell I'd talked to him that night."

"It might not have made any difference."

"No, but you never know."

"Did you hear me come in?"

"No, but you sure made a racket with those shutters. What are you doing?"

"Waiting for Pillot, actually. We're supposed to pack Edward's clothes tonight." I leaned out the window. "Edward was a pretty good athlete if he could scramble in and out of here even with the fire escape. We're three stories up." I hoped Harry wouldn't connect the noisy window and the silent door.

"Odd, isn't it?"

"What?"

"How Edward died. He was a mean drunk but not clumsy. He fell in the river. So what? He could have swum to the bank."

I was tempted to tell Harry that Edward was scared of the water and unable to swim, then discarded the idea.

"There was a nasty cut on the side of Edward's head," he continued.

"Oh? I didn't notice."

"We found it when we tried to revive him."

"He could have hit his head on the stonework along the bank." Harry looked dubious. "Or the current might have washed him into the piling."

"Or someone hit him over the head and pushed him in."

"Any number of people might have done that."

"The agent who helped me with Edward has been transferred," Harry said. "Did Pillot inform you?"

"Today?"

"Uh-huh. Special duty — in Marseilles. He stopped to say good-by around two."

"Either there's an emergency in Marseilles or Pillot wants to get rid of him."

"And it occurred to me — " Pillot chose that second to make an entrance.

"You're early, mademoiselle," he said reproachfully. "We had agreed on nine."

"Anna and I are curious about the autopsy report on Edward," Harry interjected. "Were the doctors able to determine the cause of death?"

"That was never in doubt, was it, monsieur? He drowned."

"You seem confident that it was a simple accident," I remarked.

"Blythe wasn't drunk when he left the café," Pillot replied. "He was a young man in excellent condition. If he'd been attacked, I am sure he could have defended himself."

"Yet he was drunk enough to fall in the river and drown," Harry objected.

"*Voilà,* Monsieur Radford, the difficulties of absolute proof. Perhaps the shock of the cold water, feelings of guilt or remorse or futility — who knows what happened. But according to the autopsy, Edward Blythe drowned, and the injuries that you no doubt observed occurred after death. For the rest, we must await the results of the total investigation. Now, if you please, Mademoiselle Peters and I will see about Blythe's effects. *Bonsoir, monsieur.*"

"Right," said Harry, "*bonsoir.*"

"A nice man, Monsieur Radford," Pillot commented. "A man with a tender heart, I think."

"Harry's upset about Edward, even though they nearly came to blows in Paris."

"Why was that?"

"Edward drank too much and lost those beautiful manners of his."

"Anyway," Pillot said wearily, "the matter of Edward Blythe's death is now out of my hands."

"Interference from above?"

"Extenuating circumstances, you would say."

"Tangential to the facts?"

Pillot shrugged. "There are certain problems in establishing the facts. We must depend on the doctors and the laboratory."

"Like Harry, I find it hard to believe that Edward's death was accidental."

"I do not say it was, but if it's impossible to find the killer, it makes little difference how it's labeled. It might even have been suicide."

"That's an odd creed for a policeman."

"Our bureau, you must understand, is guided by political as well as other considerations."

"And expediency is the first rule of politics?"

"Beware of becoming too cynical, mademoiselle. *Eh bien,* shall we begin?"

"I'm ready. I haven't touched anything."

Pillot made a noncommittal gesture, and we began folding Edward's custom-made shirts.

"He had exquisite taste," Pillot remarked.

"With the money to indulge it."

Pillot digressed on the unique talents of Parisian tailors while we packed. Aside from a French novel that Pillot described as extremely controversial, we uncovered nothing of interest.

"We're wasting our time."

"What did you expect?"

"I wasn't optimistic. And you, mademoiselle?"

"There's something I'd like to ask."

"Yes?"

"The other night, after the Major and I left, Gabriel's house must have been searched again?"

"Certainly."

"There was a skiff moored outside. Was anything in it?"

He shook his head. "Gabriel was a clever agent and very careful."

"He was awfully convincing. I'm sorry he was killed."

"The Blythes were one complication too many. But why do you ask about the boat?"

"It struck me that Edward might have been killed there. Moonrise was late that night. It was still dark around one or two. Edward might have examined the boat to see if Gabriel had forgotten anything. When he pulled the skiff to shore, someone slugged him and shoved him into the water. It wouldn't have taken long, and no one would notice fishermen there."

"You forget that the head injury occurred after death."

"And you forget that Edward Blythe couldn't swim."

"Where did you learn that?"

"From his governess. Not only that, he had an irrational fear of water. It might have been sufficient to push him in, especially if he wasn't sober."

Pillot looked serious and rather sad. "Have you someone in mind?"

"Yes."

"With a motive?"
"And opportunity, too."
"And proof?"
"Only circumstantial, unless you're hiding a witness."
"I advise you, mademoiselle, not to proceed with this."
"It's not really in my interest to do so."
"I will be candid with you: there is no advantage in a criminal prosecution unless it is against Major Smith. The Blythes don't matter. Smith does. Despite his escape, the Major won't be conducting any more business in France. His cover is blown and his network, as well. Naturally, this is causing embarrassing problems for some people — as always happens when corruption is made public. I have no doubt that your government will request a congressional inquiry and that there will be several courts-martial." A look of disgust appeared on his thin, ascetic face. "There is no desire," he continued, "to broaden the scandal."

"New World Oil will be grateful."
"But not you, personally?"
"Nor you, either, I think."
"I've settled for success, mademoiselle," he answered dryly.
"Can I rely on you?"
"On one condition."
"Which is?"
"You don't inform Crystal and the others that the investigation is closed. At least, not until we leave Paris. Otherwise, the deal is off."

Pillot gave me a fleeting smile. "My intentions precisely." We shook hands.

\*

Three days later I rang the bell of the town house in the Roule. A heavyset woman in a navy dress answered the door.

*"Je suis* Anna Peters *de* New World Oil. Crystal Blythe, *s'il vous plaît."*

*"Ah, un moment, mademoiselle."* She went back into the house and called Agent X, who recognized me, and apologized

for the delay. "Orders," she said in her heavy Alsatian accent.
*"Il n'y a pas de quoi."*

*"Entrez, entrez, mademoiselle,"* the housekeeper commanded, leading me into the living room.

"Hello, Miss Peters." Jared Morgan stood by the couch, a large Saint Laurent dress box in his hands.

"Hello, Jared. I'm glad to see you."

"I'm on my way out. Last-minute errands," he explained. "Crystal has a lot of them." He juggled the box, and we shook hands.

"It's good you're here. I'm sure you've been a great comfort to her."

"I've tried, but I'm still in shock. I just can't believe it."

"I'm so very sorry, Jared. How is Crystal?"

He lowered his voice. "It's been rough, but she'll be okay once she gets home. Did you know I'm going with her?"

That surprised me.

"It'll work out," he assured me. "She needs a friend she can trust to look after her interests until she's herself again. New World Oil has its concerns to protect, and Mrs. Blythe has her own troubles. I don't want Crystal to be alone."

Poor Jared. "Crystal's lucky to have such a good friend."

He blushed. "There's nothing in the world I wouldn't do for her. Well, I'd better return this."

"We'll see you at the plane."

"Crystal's upstairs. Don't be upset if she seems a little — withdrawn."

"I won't."

A beautiful bouquet of yellow roses sat on the desk. I supposed Jared had brought them. He deserved better, but he'd never believe that.

Agent X reappeared. "Mademoiselle will see you upstairs," she announced.

I climbed the spiral staircase to Crystal's room. "Hello, Crystal. I dropped by to bring you the airline tickets."

Her expression was glacial; she didn't pretend unless it was necessary. I liked that. "I was expecting a messenger."

I placed the envelope on her bureau. "I wanted to see how you're doing."

"I'll be fine."

"Good. I ran into Jared downstairs."

"He's flying home with us."

"So he said. That's kind of him."

Crystal shrugged. "He's in love with me."

"He's very nice."

She gave me a sly look. She knew she could have her pick. "Why not give him a break?" I asked, annoyed.

"Meaning?"

"You shouldn't encourage false hopes."

"I can hardly be blamed for someone's hopes. Anyway, it's none of your business."

"None at all, but it wouldn't cost you anything to be decent to him. He's crazy about you, and you're going to break his heart."

"You're paid to worry about me," she said in a cold, strained voice, "not my friends. If you'd been that concerned about Edward — "

Crystal Blythe lost right there. I'd come with half a mind to let her off the hook, but she didn't deserve charity — not at my expense. I sat down on a late Louis chair and took out the trust agreement Gilson's courier had delivered that morning. "To business, then. This has to be signed."

She threw the papers on her bed. "I've already informed those slimy lawyers that I'm not signing anything. Gilson better get them off my back. I'm competent to handle my own affairs."

"You're competent, but you don't have any experience in business. Bertrand Gilson wants to remain as your trustee for five more years. During that time, you could work at New World Oil and learn the business properly."

"All I need to know is how to sign the checks."

"You don't have any idea of your responsibilities, Crystal. Your fortune doesn't affect just you, it affects lives and jobs all down the line. That kind of wealth can't be treated frivolously."

"Don't talk to me about responsibilities and decency. Edward hasn't even been buried yet, and you're badgering me to sign away control. You're in a rush, aren't you, because once I'm home, I'll have my own lawyers to advise me."

"If you don't sign, you won't go home." I laid the monkey pendant on her desk. She gasped and reached for it.

"No. You get it when the papers are signed and witnessed."

"That's blackmail! I won't do it!"

"Think again. I'm offering you the secure management of investments that your ignorance will squander, and I'm offering you the freedom to return home as a charming, beautiful, and eligible heiress. If that prospect doesn't appeal to you, consider this one: a scandal, a French jail, and more headaches than you've ever dreamed could exist. I don't particularly care, Crystal. You're careless about other people, and selfish and overconfident. Why should I have risked my life and endangered a friend just to do you a favor? Sign this, and I get the credit. Don't sign, and I'll have the satisfaction of telling Pillot exactly what happened in Strasbourg. One is as good as the other as far as I'm concerned."

"You can't intimidate me. If Pillot suspected me he'd have questioned me further in Strasbourg." Her tone was sharp, but I noticed the anxiety in her eyes.

"I found the pendant along the riverbank the night Edward died. You could have lost it earlier, but I think you'll concede that my theory is plausible. Edward climbed out the window early in the evening. At about midnight, Harry thought he heard Edward return, and he came to my room to tell me. Your radio was on, so we both assumed you and Edward were in. But we were mistaken: the noise Harry heard was you leaving. He misinterpreted your exit because you had oiled the locks and hinges of your door and Edward's. You went out to meet Edward, probably because you wanted a private conversation with him where you couldn't be overheard as I had overheard you two arguing in the living room. Obviously, I've no idea what you talked about, but I do know this: Edward couldn't swim."

Crystal turned pale and shifted in her chair. "You would be one of the few people to know about his fear of the water.

"You two quarreled — Edward wasn't exactly reasonable when he drank — maybe there was a struggle, but somehow Edward wound up in the river. I think you shoved him in."

"That's a lie! I loved Edward. It's not true!"

"Perhaps. But the next part is true. You returned to your room, got into your nightgown, switched off the radio, and pretended to look for Edward — in my room. That was a clever touch, I admit. By the time we found him, he'd drowned. If you'd called for help right away, he'd be alive today. And you'd have only half that money to spend."

"It isn't the money. I don't give a damn about the money!"

Her voice was anguished, and I believed her: it wasn't the money.

"I didn't hurt him. There's no proof. You're making this up. They can't arrest me."

"Crystal, I'm convinced that, directly or indirectly, you're responsible for Edward's death. If I confront Monsieur Pillot with the pendant, he'll have to take action, and a diligent search is likely to produce witnesses who overheard you two arguing or who noticed you in the area that night. And another thing: that pair of damp sneakers in your closet. They're in a plastic bag in my suitcase. A lab report on them might be instructive."

Crystal didn't react. Her eyes were tormented, but she was tough when it counted. I dropped the pendant into my shoulder bag. "You're gambling and you're going to lose," I said. "My honest opinion is that if the scandal breaks, Pillot will have no choice but to conduct a thorough investigation, not the pro forma job he laid on us. And if that happens, the best you can hope for are nasty rumors you'd never live down. At worst, you're risking a murder indictment."

Downstairs, the housekeeper rattled some pots, and a small dog began yapping monotonously in the garden. Finally Crystal asked, "Do you think Edward was to blame for Gaby's death?"

I weighed my answer. "My hunch is that Edward wanted to get rid of Gabriel, and he focused the Major's attention on him as a gunrunner. But unless Edward realized that Gabriel was a French agent, his information was not crucial."

She shook her head. "I doubt that he knew."

"Only the Major knows, and he's unlikely to tell."

"I had to know for sure." There was pain in her voice.

"We can't always be sure about the people we love. You and Edward expected too much from each other."

"Edward believed what he chose to believe. No matter what the facts were, he'd stick to his own concept of himself. Lying wasn't deliberate with him; that's why it was so difficult to separate the truth from his fantasies."

I nodded, but Crystal paid no attention to me. She was rehearsing the chain of events in her own mind, just as Edward would have done.

"I tried to pry the truth out of him. He insisted that he'd only told the Major that Gabriel belonged to a terrorist group. We had a fight, as you guessed, and when he left his room I followed, even though I was scared to climb out the window. Anyway, I met him at the locks. He'd had quite a few drinks by the time I caught up with him, and he'd gotten it into his head that there had to be evidence at Gabriel's house that would substantiate everything he'd told me. I thought that was ridiculous, but he insisted on searching the house. He kept repeating, 'I'll prove it to you, you'll see,' until I agreed. The house was locked, so he decided to break a window. I was almost ready to believe him — I really wanted to — but he was always such a convincing actor. I had to be positive, don't you see?"

I nodded again, afraid to interrupt her train of thought.

"The skiff was tied up near the house. I told Edward that if he got in the boat and swore that he didn't have anything to do with Gabriel's death I would believe him. He turned white. 'You want to kill me,' he said, without thinking, but he hauled the boat to shore. There was water in the bottom of it, like ink, and Edward got in. He let it drift out, and then he stood up on one of the seats. That scared me. I begged him to sit down. 'No, Edward, please,' I said. 'Don't do that.' He started laughing

— or crying. Obviously he was terrified, and I pleaded with him to stop. He screamed, 'I wanted him dead,' 'I wanted him dead.' Then he lost his balance, the boat tipped, and he fell into the water. He never came back up." Crystal stared straight ahead and became again for an instant the person I'd seen that night along the Ill.

"Why didn't you run for help?" I asked as gently as I could.

"I panicked. There was no chance to rescue him. I felt as if I'd lost half myself, as though I'd walked into a buzz saw and been sliced in two." She recovered after a moment. "The current is strong there. I ran along the water under the bridge, but he was gone."

"That's where I found the pendant."

"The catch must have broken. I wasn't aware I'd lost it until later. It was my favorite thing. Edward bought it for my fifth birthday." She gave a soft, unhappy laugh. "Right after the other accident."

"The other accident?"

"Right. Mother didn't tell you about that, did she? She took Edward out in a rowboat. Drunk, of course. He nearly drowned. I was on the shore and saw everything."

That explained a lot but not enough. Crystal offered nothing more, and finally I said, "Still, I don't understand why you failed to get help, why you concealed all this."

"It was too late to make any difference — "

"It could have made a difference to you. Had you explained what happened, we would have believed you."

"Don't you believe me now?"

"Yes." But like Crystal, I needed assurance. There were too many loose ends, and any one of them might unravel her whole story. "You've placed yourself in an untenable position, though. You would have a lot of explaining to do to a prosecutor."

"It was an accident! It wasn't my fault!"

"Crystal, you bear some responsibility for what's happened. Don't make believe, like Edward. There's no future in it."

She leaned back in her chair and resumed the courteous,

controlled Blythe manner. "Don't worry about me. I can take care of myself."

She had no intention of winding up like her brother. She had the nerves, all right; guilt was for other people.

"What, now, Anna?" she asked, as if the answer were a foregone conclusion.

Was it her maddening self-deception or a sordid profit motive that goaded me? "My original offer is a fair one. It still stands."

She sat bolt upright, furious. "Damn you. You've tricked me, but I'll deny everything."

"You're deceiving yourself, Crystal, and you're a fool if you don't accept my offer. I'm giving you a second chance. If I were very moral, I'd call Pillot right now. If I were corrupt, I'd demand a six-figure retainer. You're lucky: I'm only semicorrupt. All I'm asking is your name on a deal that will benefit you in the long run."

She made a number of threats that I assumed she meant. Then she offered me money; I declined.

"You're wasting your time, Crystal. Like you, I need some insurance."

"Do you seriously think I'd try to hurt you? I'm not vindictive. I'm — "

I shook my head. "You wouldn't give Jared a break, and he's one of your oldest friends. You flunked the test. Now sign these papers."

She hesitated, then picked up the pen.

"I'll call for a notary and witnesses."

"What about Jared and your friend Harry?" she asked maliciously.

I ignored her and lifted the receiver.

"You owe me the pendant — and the shoes."

"As soon as you sign." I dialed the café two blocks away, where Unwin, Morby, and a skinny notary in a perfumed wig waited for my call.

# Chapter 15

"Is it all going to fit up there?"

"I think so. Hold this a second, would you?" Harry passed down a long, fat mailing tube of prints and posters he'd collected along the Left Bank and shoved several more packages into the overhead luggage compartment.

Three rows ahead, Crystal and Jared sat together. She wore a dark summer suit and stared moodily out of the window. Jared glanced at her shyly from time to time. He reminded me of a child carrying something beautiful and fragile that is sure to smash and disappoint him. It had been awkward meeting them. Crystal had complained to him about the agreement, and he was disillusioned with me. I hoped that I wouldn't have to see either of them again.

"What did you give Crystal and Jared back in the lobby?" I asked as Harry dropped into his seat.

"A couple of sketches. I drew both her and Edward while we were in Strasbourg. I thought she might like the one of her brother, and when Jared saw it, he asked for Crystal's."

"That was kind of you. They're excellent."

Harry fiddled with his seat belt. "Anna?"

"Yes?"

"Did Crystal sign an agreement with New World?"

Damn artists notice too much. "Yes, as a matter of fact she did. It should work out very much to her advantage."

"She told the lawyers she'd never sign."

"They didn't have a smart approach. Gilson was right after all: it *was* a job that required a woman's touch."

"You're kidding."

"Not entirely."

He watched the stewardess demonstrating the oxygen equipment. "Did you have to force her to sign?"

"Let's just say it was the best of unattractive alternatives."

"I see."

"Don't act like that. You didn't have to make the decision."

He didn't answer. Instead, he opened his sketchbook and handed me a pencil drawing. It was a beautifully finished double portrait of the Blythes. Edward was sitting in a carved wooden chair at the Place Kléber and Crystal was balanced on the arm, leaning against his shoulder. They were at once lovely and sinister.

"Is it a likeness?"

"Yes, unfortunately."

"What did you say to Gilson?"

"That some day Crystal would prove a formidable addition to the Board of Directors."

"That's all?"

"That's all. I could hardly tell the chairman of the board that he'd better start running scared."